Russell is happy to help his renters from a distance. That is, until he learns their true identity.

It was too late by the time he spotted her. Busy thinking about what more he could do for Mutt, Russell hadn't paid attention. Monday morning, he went out the front door and nearly knocked over the girl. "Whoa!" He instinctively grabbed her arms to keep her from tumbling backward.

She let out a gasp, then got her footing. Color flooded her cheeks even though he released her. "Excuse me. I brought you this." She nudged the basket into his arms and stepped back. "Your list. . .tools and wood and things. . ." She nervously moistened her lips. "I thought you might want it back."

He nodded curtly.

"I–I heard a woofing sound when I came the other day. There is a bone for your dog."

His chin came up. *She's been spying on me.*

"Thank you for the firewood and the porch." She'd inched back toward the steps, and the morning sun glinted on her pale hair and a necklace—a very plain, rather small, silver cross. "It is very kind of you to help us, Sir." He gave no reply, so she whispered, "Good-bye."

As she walked off, Russell stared at her back and felt a bolt of hatred nearly consume him. *She's German.*

CATHY MARIE HAKE is a Southern California native who loves her work as a nurse and Lamaze teacher. She and her husband have a daughter, a son, and a dog, so life is never dull or quiet. Cathy considers herself a sentimental packrat, collecting antiques and Hummel figurines. She otherwise keeps busy with reading, writing, baking, and being a prayer warrior. "I am easily distracted during prayer, so I devote certain tasks and chores to specific requests or persons so I can keep faithful in my prayer life."

Books by Cathy Marie Hake

HEARTSONG PRESENTS
HP370—Twin Victories
HP481—Unexpected Delivery
HP512—Precious Burdens
HP545—Love is Patient
HP563—Redeemed Hearts
HP583—Ramshackle Rose

Restoration

Cathy Marie Hake

Heartsong Presents

A note from the Author:
I love to hear from my readers! You may correspond with me by writing:

Cathy Marie Hake
Author Relations
PO Box 719
Uhrichsville, OH 44683

ISBN 1-59310-106-6

RESTORATION

Our mission is to publish and distribute inspirational products offering exceptional value and biblical encouragement to the masses.

All Scripture quotations are taken from the King James Version of the Bible.

PRINTED IN THE U.S.A.

one

Virginia, 1918

Tonight, when they're asleep, I'll burn it. Russell Diamond stared at his uniform in the drawer. He hadn't intended to find it, but now that he'd stumbled across it, Russell was certain of the action he had to take. No one would have to know—at least, not for a long while. By then, maybe he'd have the words to smooth over the whole situation.

The olive drabs looked so innocuous, all pressed and clean—just as they had the day he'd first put them on. By the time he got home, the uniform still held blood, mud, and sweat as well as sea salt from the quick "laundering" it was given aboard the passenger liner the army used to transport the wounded back from Le Havre. Russell loved his country, but he hated war. He wanted no reminder of what he'd seen and done. For now, he took care to glide the bottom drawer of the walnut wardrobe shut and headed for the backyard.

Not many folks had an orchard for a backyard. Big, old, beautiful peach and apricot trees near the house gave way to younger apple trees farther away. Dad planted a dozen of the apples the year he and Mom married—mostly because he didn't care for the taste of peaches.

Mom and Dad sat on the porch swing, sipping lemonade and enjoying the sunset. Russell didn't feel like talking, so he bobbed a curt nod and plowed on past them. His leg ached as he limped at his best speed. He knew he should have been warmer to his parents, but it wasn't in him. Instead of ruining their pleasant evening, he'd go off on his own. Snagging a pair of buckets and slipping out of sight, he hoped they'd assume he was off to weed a bit.

Among the trees, with peach, apricot, and nectarine blossoms drifting down on him in a gentle Virginia breeze, Russell sat on the ground and jerked weeds until the first pail overflowed. He set it aside and collected more to fill the second. The pain in his leg intensified, but he kept working. Coming across a withered apple core, Russell pitched it into the bucket with the bitter knowledge that he'd missed harvest this past year.

It was too late—or far too early, he thought wryly, for even gathering any windfall. Mom always took the bird-pecked or bruised fruit and turned it into sweet cider, cinnamon applesauce, peach jam. . .something. She could find the good in even the worst of situations. *But she was never in war.*

Russell continued to scan for weeds. Anything—anything to keep him busy so he wouldn't have to think.

He finally sat and leaned against a tree his father had planted the Sunday after Russell's birth. At twenty, it was vibrant and straight; a contrast to the dried up, gnarled way Russell felt inside. Home was just the same as always—Dad working at Diamond Emporium, Mom busy with charitable tasks and cooking far too much food. Sis had married one of Buttonhole's fine young men, and they'd be blessed with a baby in a few months. Folks visited over picket fences with their neighbors, bachelors still had a special pew at the back of the sanctuary, and old Mrs. Blanchard still missed about every fifth or sixth note as she played the piano in her parlor.

But I've changed. I'm different. I'll never be the same.

Pain rolled over him again. Russell closed his eyes and let his head fall back against the rough bark. Minutes passed, memories swelled. Everything suddenly shifted when a soft footstep sounded. Russell jolted and grabbed for a rifle that wasn't there.

"Son."

"Dad." He rasped that single word and tried to act casual as he pulled his arm back into his lap, but his heart still thundered.

Dad's step faltered; then he sauntered the last fifteen yards or so, weaving past trees. *He can't stride through his own orchard because of me—I've taken away the pleasure he always took in his evening strolls.*

In days gone by, Dad would have reached out to give a fatherly squeeze to Russell's shoulder, but he'd learned sudden moves and sounds set Russell on edge, so he didn't venture any form of touch. Russell ached for the missing contact.

"Your mother and I would like to talk with you."

"Yes, Sir." *The time's come.* Russell got to his feet and walked in silence beside Dad until they reached the back porch. *Dad's slowing his pace to compensate for my limp.* Russell resented the need for it.

Mom, her hair in its usual mussed bun and her apron slightly askew, patted the seat of the porch swing next to her. He sat there, and she handed him a glass of lemonade.

"Thanks, Mom."

Russell could feel her studying him in the waning light. Dad set to lighting a lamp. Unable to look them in the eyes, Russell watched his father's hands as he performed the simple task. Once done, Dad sat on an old wooden chair.

"You're hurting, Son—and I'm not talking about your leg."

Russell shifted his gaze and stared at a droplet of water meandering down the side of his glass. His father's quiet words were so typical of him—direct, open, and unadorned. The very stark quality of them made the truth all that much more painful. The distraction of watching such a mundane thing allowed Russell to consider a response. Finally, he opted for honesty. "Yes."

"We knew going away would. . .be hard on you." Mom practiced no artifice, and her candor and sincerity had been qualities he'd come to admire very early on. It tore at him that she felt the need to measure her words so carefully.

Until this evening, he hadn't known she'd also been watching her actions just as cautiously. Mom hadn't washed and hung his uniform back in his wardrobe; she'd laundered it and quietly slipped it away in the bottom of the wardrobe in Sis's old room. If he hadn't been looking for the battered old valise they kept in the drawer, he wouldn't have seen the painstakingly folded olive drab pants and shirt just awhile ago.

Russell chugged down the lemonade, mostly because it bought him a few more moments. He set aside the glass, then looked from one parent to the other. "I mean no disrespect. This is hard." He drew in a deep breath. "I can't stay here anymore."

Mom wrapped both of her arms around his right arm and leaned her head on his shoulder. She was holding on tight, just as she had the evening before he took the train to leave as a soldier. "You haven't finished healing yet. The cast just came off. Wait. Stay just a little while until you're more stable."

He'd known she'd resist his plan, but Russell still knew what he had to do. Dad searched his eyes, and Russell couldn't take the scrutiny. He looked away and subtly shook his head. Waiting was out of the question.

"Have you prayed about it?" His father's face had looked drawn.

Russell couldn't lie, even though he knew the truth would burden them. He'd not taken the matter to God—in fact, he and the Almighty were on very shaky terms. "No."

Mom gasped, and Russell knew he'd let her down. Her voice

showed it when she finally said in a strained tone, "Aw, Honey."

Mom's faith was deep and dear to her; he'd strayed from the path of righteousness. It was one of the biggest reasons he couldn't live here.

"You should still stay, Russell." She rubbed her cheek on his shoulder. "It takes time when a man's been hurt for his body and soul to settle with all he's gone through. We understand. It doesn't change how we feel about you."

Russell gently separated from her and stood. He and his father exchanged a momentary look—one that silently agreed to shield Mom from as much of the pain as they could. Russell dipped his head and pressed a kiss on her hair. "I love you, too." The scent of peaches and cloves that always clung to her gave him a scrap of comfort.

Dad took a deep breath and let it out slowly. "We have something else to discuss."

Though he wanted to escape to the solitude of his bedroom, Russell forced himself to sit back down on the swing. One last night, he'd sit here. He'd discipline himself to pretend things weren't so bad. It was the least he could do.

"A letter came today," Dad said. "My great-uncle Timothy passed on. The family house belonged to him. He boarded up the place, and no one's lived in it for several years. The day we learned you were coming home, he wrote his will and left the house and all of his wealth to you, Russell."

"Money won't cure what ails me."

"No, it won't." Dad sighed. "And I'm glad you have the wisdom to see that, but you said you need to leave. You'll always have a place to come back to here, but in the meantime, you have a home and funds to take care of yourself."

Russell nodded. Words seemed futile, and Mom seemed far too fragile.

Mom tilted her head and looked up at him. She tried her

best to give him a brave smile even though tears glossed her eyes. "Think on this more. Sleep on it. Your dad and I will pray." Pain radiated from her as she added, "If you still feel you have to go, we'll be supportive."

They all sat together as night engulfed the yard. Crickets chirped and cicadas whirred. The wind soughed through the branches. He'd left as a boy and come back a man—but for this one evening, Russell relished the one thing that he'd not been stripped of: the unvarnished, uncomplicated, unconditional love of his family.

If he stayed here, the ache in his soul would ruin that. He knew he had to go.

ʔ

Crack! Lorelei Goetz looked down at the two pieces of glass in her hand and grimaced. They hadn't broken along the line she'd scored. Setting down the smaller segment, she focused her attention on the larger. If she tapped it a bit more with the ball end of her scoring tool, she might still get the cut.

Minuscule glass slivers caught the sunlight pouring in through her workroom window, turning the edge of her table into a kaleidoscope of red, gold, and blue. She paused for a second to appreciate the prisms the clear shards added to the mix. Papa had called them the beams of joy. He'd taught her the art of stained glass, and, at times like this, it was bittersweet to see the beauty but not have him here to share it.

"You start early today, *Ja?*"

Lorelei looked over her shoulder and smiled. *"Ja,* Mama. I'd like to finish this window a few days early if I can. Mr. Grun said he'd be going to Portsmouth next week, and he'd be willing to deliver it for me."

He mother smiled and nodded. *"Wunderbar!* He will be very careful. Herr Grun is a kind man."

Lorelei turned back to the glass. "Yes, Mama, he is." She

paused a moment, then added in a firm tone, "It doesn't mean I'm going to pack up and go marry his cousin in South Dakota. This is our home—yours and mine. We're staying here."

Mama clucked her tongue. "You are a pretty girl, my Lori. There is no reason for you to spend your days breaking glass and putting it back together when you could be married and having babies. Your papa would want you to."

"Yes," Lorelei agreed pensively. "Papa would have been a wonderful grandpa."

Taking advantage of the opening, her mother rushed to add, "I was married and had you by the time I was your age."

"Twenty isn't old, Mama, and Papa also wanted me to find a man who would love me the way he loved you. He told me not to settle on anything less than a perfect fit—not in a window, not in my marriage."

"If only he were here. He would talk sense into you. There is a difference between wishes and wisdom, Lori."

She turned around. "Mama, what's wrong?"

Her mother came into the workroom and perched on a wooden stool. She looked like a chickadee—a plump, compact woman with brown and gray hair; she wore a faded gray apron over a brown and black dress. Instead of folding her arms as she'd normally do, she shoved them into the apron pocket—a sure sign she was worried. Instead of speaking, she shrugged.

Lorelei set down the glass, blew on her hands to remove any glass slivers, then went to her mother. "Mama, we have each other."

"But we have little else!" Her mother blurted out the words, then bit her lip.

"You're worried about money?"

"Yes, but more—I'm worried about you. So many still look at us as the enemy."

The injustice of that hurt. Papa went to fight for America, yet because they had German ancestors, still spoke German at home, and had a German last name, folks reviled them. It wasn't until after Papa died and the government sent a soldier in a fancy uniform to give them shiny medals in Papa's honor that many of the townspeople finally shifted from hostility to wariness.

"There are hard feelings—ones that won't fade for a long time. Too many of the young men refuse to be seen with a German girl even just for a date. They won't want you for a wife." Mama pasted on a smile. "If you go to South Dakota, you will have a husband and children."

"Arranged marriages ended in the Dark Ages. I'm happy here with you. We'll just pray that if God has a husband in mind for me, He'll bring him to our doorstep."

Mama shook her head. "What am I to do with you? Men are not like bottles of milk that get delivered to your porch."

Lorelei laughed and gave her mother a peck on the cheek. "Last Sunday, the pastor told us to seek God's will and to pray specifically, in faith."

Mama finally pulled her hands out of her apron pocket and rubbed her legs. "Child, I'm going to end up with flat knees from all of the hours I spend kneeling in prayer for you."

two

"Son." His father's voice carried grim determination. "I want a promise from you."

Russell stood near the backyard porch steps, by the barrel Mom grew strawberries in. He plucked a dried leaf from one of the plants. Mom was inside, putting together some food for him to take. From how red and puffy her eyes had looked at breakfast, he knew she'd been up half the night weeping. He'd come out here because. . .well, because.

"You write your mom. Let her know how you're doing."

Swallowing hard, Russell lifted his chin and stared at Dad. He gave a curt nod. "You have my word."

"And you have my word that if you need me, I'll be there. If it would help, I'm ready to come along right now—just me. I have a sense that you're fighting mightily to shield Mom from things."

Knocking the heel of his hand against the barrel, Russell cleared his throat. Dad had built the emporium from a failing, little, backwater shop into a thriving concern. For him to be willing to leave it all at the drop of a hat underscored the love he felt. "Dad, I appreciate the offer, but you were right last night. I have to be alone."

"Son, you're not alone; God is with you."

"I told you last night—I'm not talking to God anymore."

"I heard you." His dad came down the steps and plucked a strawberry. He dusted it off gently and popped it into his mouth.

He chose the fresh, sweet berry; I'm standing here clutching the dead leaf. Russell let out a bitter laugh.

Dad shoved his hands in his pockets and didn't take offense at Russell's mirthless reaction. "It's not your leg that's troubling you; it's the ugliness you endured. It's a soldier's burden, one I hoped you'd be spared. Your great-uncle Tim was battle scarred and struggled mightily with his feelings and his faith."

"I don't remember much of him—just that he didn't get married until he was real old."

"He took what little was left of the family shipping business after the war and threw himself into rebuilding it. Business and the sea were his lifeblood, but his escape—his refuge— was the old family house."

"He left it."

"Originally, he went back home after the war. With time, he finally found peace there. When his wife developed consumption, the doctor recommended they move. It wasn't until then he left. You'll find peace there, Son. I have faith."

"I heard old Mr. Sibony has a matched pair of geldings he wants to sell." Russell hoped his father would go along with the change of subject. "I figure I'll just ride to the coast."

Shortly thereafter, with a blanket tied to the rear of his saddle and packs tied to the second gelding, Russell left Buttonhole. Following the directions he'd been given, he rode for two days until he passed through a seaside town and arrived at the outskirts where the road branched off. To the right, he spotted a charming little cottage with two chimneys, a budding garden, and sheets on the clothesline, snapping in the stiff breeze. That breeze also carried a woman's voice.

He didn't want to deal with others, so instead of following the curving dirt road, he cut across a spread that once must have been a well-kept lawn. He could see stables in the distance off another fork of the road, but ahead loomed the old Newcomb house.

Russell halted the horses near a clump of overgrown

shrubs and studied the house. He listened intently for any sounds of inhabitants and heard none. Not a single track or footprint marred the earth. Satisfied the place hadn't been approached from this direction, he tethered the geldings and reconnoitered on foot.

He continued to scan the ground for signs of footprints and the windows for faces or moving curtains. Several of the windows were cracked. A few panes were missing entirely. What glass remained intact looked murky with age-old, undisturbed dust. *Good. No one's been here.*

Water would be his most basic need, so he strode down a weed-encrusted cobblestone path to a well. Someone had wisely fitted a cover over the well for safety's sake. Russell nodded approvingly. He dragged it to the side, looked about for a rope and bucket, and realized neither was present. Inhaling deeply, he could smell the sweet, damp aroma of fresh water. He flipped a small stone in and heard a satisfying splash.

Russell made his way to the front of the house and allowed himself to look up and assess the architecture. It must have once been a graceful place—a large antebellum mansion meant for rearing a big family. It would accommodate sizable crowds, and from family stories he'd heard, the Newcombs had done considerable entertaining.

The roof lacked a plethora of shingles, warning Russell the inside undoubtedly suffered water damage. Some of the upper story's windows were cracked; a few were even missing. The ground floor windows had been boarded up, and sections of clapboard on the seaward side of the house looked thoroughly rotten. The veranda sagged here and there.

It looks like I feel.

Dad had told him his great-uncle had found refuge here after the ravages of the War Between the States. *It can be my hideaway now, too. There's plenty of work to be done, and it doesn't matter how long it takes.*

Russell trod carefully—not just because of his leg, but because the steps and veranda sported broken or missing planks. He curled his hands around a gray, weathered board and yanked. Nails squealed, and the piece pulled free. After that, he pried two more slashes of wood free and revealed a leaded glass window. Russell rubbed dirt from the panes and peered inside.

Cloth lay over a lump he presumed to be a piece of furniture, looking like a gray-shrouded ghost. This had to be the foyer. *How did I imagine I'd find refuge in this desolate old place?*

Russell plotted a course across the veranda and yanked several boards down from across the front door. Whoever drove the nails in had meant them to stay. It took considerable effort to clear the door. When revealed, the entrance boasted a matching pair of panels that bore elegant carvings of dogwood blossoms. The doors showed no evidence of a lock, but Russell still expected significant resistance when he simultaneously twisted and pushed both door handles. To his great surprise, though, the doors groaned loudly, then swung open with ease.

Russell forced himself not to press against the doorway, to pan across the foyer with his rifle. The fact that he didn't have his rifle had a lot to do with why he refrained from the action. The habits he'd developed to survive had become ingrained. Russell wondered if he'd ever get over feeling the need to exercise such extreme vigilance. He entered the house, then closed the doors behind himself.

And promptly sneezed.

The sound echoed up the great wooden staircase, into all of the rooms, and died out. Dust, inches thick, covered every surface in sight. Not a footprint marred the floors; no handprints disturbed the stair rails or doorsills. Enveloped in nothing but dust and silence, Russell closed his eyes and let his shoulders slump. At least he'd found the solitude he craved.

❧

"It's beautiful," Mama said in a hushed voice as she looked at the nearly finished window on Lorelei's worktable.

Lorelei painstakingly rubbed one of the hand-painted segments with a soft, cotton rag. She'd spent hours on that one piece because the angel's wings needed to convey the shelter of God's provision of protection. "I'm happy with the way it turned out."

"Your papa would be so proud."

Lorelei ached as she heard the tears in her mother's voice. The pain of losing him was still fresh. "It makes me feel close to him, working on these windows. I sent him a sketch of this one in my last letter."

Mama hugged her. They huddled close in the workshop, surrounded by a pair of sturdy tables, frames, lead cames, pieces of glass, and assorted tools of the trade. Papa loved working on church windows, and they both felt surrounded by echoes of his love whenever they were in the workshop.

When Papa went to war, they couldn't afford to stay in town. Rent was too high. Then, too, having a German last name and accent didn't exactly make them welcome. A friend of Lorelei's told them about this cottage. Lorelei had walked out to it that very day, looked over the little cottage, and decided it would suit their needs admirably. As far as she was concerned, the workshop cinched the deal.

She found the attorney who handled the property, and he'd gotten special permission from the old man who owned the place to rent it. The rent was ridiculously low, and Lorelei suspected it was a move of compassionate pity; but since the budget looked grim and orders for windows were slow, she'd thanked God and signed the papers for a long-term lease.

She'd worried she'd lose that special feeling of being close to Papa when they moved, but her fears were unfounded. Even Mama, after they'd settled the last soldering rod into place, remarked that it all felt "right."

"Did you know," Mama whispered in a tight voice, "after we lost Johann, Junior, your papa painted his face for an angel in the church window?"

Lorelei gave her mother a playful squeeze. "Not until he and I went to Richmond to install another window at that church. I saw it and asked Papa why he painted my pesky brother as an angel."

Mama pushed away and clucked her tongue in her special way that she tried to use to induce shame.

"You're not fooling me, Mama. You only make that sound when you know you'll end up laughing if you talk!"

"Oh, my Lori." Mama reached up and patted Lorelei's cheek. "You are God's gift to me. When the shadows of life fall across my heart, you cast them away with your sunny laugh."

"Let's hope my laugh lasts long enough for us to run out and get the sheets off the line. It looks like we're about to get a spring shower!"

They scampered outside. Lorelei ran ahead while her mother grabbed the wicker laundry basket. By the time Mama met her by the clothesline, she'd gathered the slips and underwear they'd made from carefully bleached flour sacks and pillowcases. Lorelei dumped them into the basket, then started whipping the clothespins off one end of the sheet while Mama dislodged them from the other. Ocean winds were unreliable and often grew brisk enough to sweep any unsecured items right off the line, so they'd learned to secure everything—just in case.

She and Mama had the simple chore down to a quick

routine. She matched the two bottom corners while Mama matched the two top ones. They'd snap the sheet, fold it in half lengthwise again, then meet in the middle. Today, as the first sprinkles hit, they dumped that sheet into the basket instead of finishing the folds.

Lorelei laughed as she skidded around the clothesline and yanked the next sheet. Her action sent clothespins pinging into the air like crickets.

"Your Sunday dress! Get it first," Mama called as she pulled her own Sunday-best black skirt free from the pins.

The skies opened up with a flash shower. They threw the last few items into the basket, each grabbed a handle, and ran to the house. Mama stared at the basket, then scowled at Lori. "In South Dakota, they would not have storms from the ocean."

"In South Dakota, they don't have sunrises over the ocean, either."

"Hmpf."

Lorelei pretended Mama's reaction was to the top layer of laundry that had gotten soggy. "I'll help you hang up whatever is still damp. I have some twine in the workshop."

"You will do more on that window. I will hang the clothes." Mama wrinkled her nose. "I'll let you do the ironing later while I read the Bible."

"I ought to have time to do that later this afternoon since God is watering the garden for us." Lorelei took a few steps closer to the window and tilted her head as if doing so would help her see around a clump of trees. "I thought I saw a man walking a horse."

"Sweetheart, no one would be out in this rain, walking a horse—riding one, maybe." Mama raised her hands, palm upward in a who-knows gesture. "But not walking it. If the horse were lame, the man would have stopped back at the Rimmons' instead of coming up this old road."

Lorelei didn't see anything more. German Americans suffered all sorts of persecution, and the newspaper habitually carried articles denouncing the "Huns." Since they'd moved out here, no one had bothered them, but Lorelei still felt wary.

"Usually, I am the one who worries," Mama teased. "I tell you, no one is out there."

"I suppose you're right." Still, Lorelei folded her arms and tried to rub away the shivery feeling that wasn't from the rain.

three

Pure, sweet, clean rain. Russell had just finished walking through the entire house, including the attic, when the spring storm hit. He'd moved from room to room, shutting doors in hopes that the stiff breeze wouldn't find too many cracks and blow the dust around that had him sneezing repeatedly. He'd have to tackle the chambers one at a time, collecting the worst of the grime before he tried to air out the house. He'd grown up doing a lot of dusting and cleaning for Dad at the emporium; he knew the routine well.

Russell headed for the kitchen, having decided that he could open the large windows and push open the door. The draft ought to race through and blast out a fair bit of the mess. An ancient straw broom in a small closet by the pantry came in handy. He used it to dislodge a pair of massive cobwebs that swagged like fishing nets from the ceiling to the stove and worktable. He'd need somewhere to set his gear, so he whisked off the tabletop and cast aside the broom.

Unsteady due to his healing leg, he loped outside toward the shrubs to fetch the geldings. "Hey, boys." The large workhorses lifted their heads and snuffled. "You've kept busy, haven't you?" Russell stroked the closest one's damp withers.

The horses didn't mind the rain in the least. From the looks of the uneven grasses, they'd satisfied themselves by foraging. "Come on. I have a place in mind for you." He'd not checked out the stable yet, and Russell refused to keep his mounts there until it was cleared out and held fresh water. The horses obediently walked along as Russell led them to an ivy-covered overhang off the one small wing near the kitchen. Half-a-dozen old, large urns lay there, tipped on their sides. Russell dumped out what little dirt remained in them, then set them upright to collect the downpour from the roof. He swiftly unburdened the first horse of the saddle and the second one of the bundles, then went back inside.

The pump in the kitchen needed to be primed, but he rather doubted it would work even then. The gaskets and cups inside must have rotted out long ago. Determined to work through the fiery pain in his leg, Russell dragged a tottering wooden chair toward the cabinets. He dropped heavily onto it, then jerked open each drawer and cupboard within reach.

A single plate. A chipped mug. A coffee can filled with mismatched knives and forks. . .battered pieces. *Like me.* He gathered them into a pile and left them when he happened along a set of large mixing bowls. Russell swiped the bowls under the water cascading from the roof, then started collecting drinking water in them.

That task accomplished, he recalled other receptacles he'd spotted during his tour. Soon, his odd collection of pans, wash pitchers, two slop jars, a metal milk pail, and a battered steel washtub sat in strategic spots throughout the house, catching leaks. It made for an odd symphony of pings, drips, and drumming sounds, but something about it took the edge off his restlessness.

Aware he couldn't clean the whole place in a single day, Russell decided to focus on the largest bedchamber upstairs. The dust nearly choked him, so he tied a kerchief over his nose and mouth, then yanked the fancy draperies from the rods. He dragged them across the floor to help get rid of a goodly portion of the grit, then dropped them over the banister into a heap on the floor of the foyer. Just that small amount of handling had the fabric disintegrating.

"What am I doing?" His words echoed in the house as he looked down at the billowing dust he'd sent into the air. "I'm not going to find peace here."

Thunder boomed over the roof.

I have nowhere else to go. May as well make this place habitable. Russell figured he'd do better to shake out a blanket or sheet and hang it over the window. He thought of the sheets he'd seen on the neighbor's clothesline and felt a pang of envy for how fresh and clean they'd be. He'd be sleeping wrapped in a blanket tonight—much as he had in the trenches.

Russell shook off that awful analogy, surveyed the room, and quickly settled on priorities. He retrieved the broom and used it to sweep down the walls. Cobwebs and dirt banished, the walls looked the same shade as the sky when it went from blue to that first tint of twilight lavender. The floor was, to his relief, sound as could be. It creaked here and there, but that didn't much matter. He could fill the spots with talcum to solve that paltry irritation.

Russell limped about, using the water collected from the leaks to sluice off the bedroom floor. He quickly swept out the tiled upstairs washroom and bathtub, then used the next round of water to do a cursory wash down of that room, too.

Clothes damp from rainwater and sweat, Russell sat on the old tub's edge. *At least no one is here to witness how weak I am.* The notion of being out of shape stuck in his craw. Tall, broad-shouldered, and well-muscled, he'd never been limited. *I refuse to give in now.* He shoved away from the tub and left the room, his uneven gait ringing like a never-ending taunt on the tiled floor.

He braced himself in the door to the hallway. *This is my haven? This? Supposedly Uncle Timothy found contentment here, but I can't see how. Maybe he was just better at fooling folks into thinking he was at peace. He left it behind as empty and forgotten as a snake leaves his old skin.*

Russell's leg ached abominably, but he refused to acknowledge it. He headed for the kitchen, opened the door, and saw the horses contentedly drinking out of the urn. He stuck his hands out into the rain, scrubbed his face, and turned back toward the house. Mom had slipped in some of those little tablets she considered to be cure-alls. He shook two of the Bayer Aspirin into his palm, shuddered at the bitter taste, and washed them down with rainwater.

Hungry, Russell unwrapped the last two slices of bread Mom had sent along. He had canned provisions as well, but for now, he didn't much care what he ate. No matter what he put in his mouth, it all tasted like sawdust. Even Mom's famous peach jam failed to give him any pleasure.

Russell looked about the kitchen and let out a deep sigh. This old place was a filthy hulk. His survey of the structure showed the roof and veranda needed immediate and extensive attention, but the rest of the house was fairly sound.

He didn't dare try to start a fire in one of the fireplaces or the stove. Even if there weren't nests in the flues or stovepipe, he didn't have much in the way of useable fuel. Then, too, the wooden structure was dry as could be. One spark, and the whole place would become a torch. He'd need to varnish, paint, and polish the place from top to bottom to protect it.

Time. It would take time—not just days or weeks, but months. That was okay with him. He had the time. He needed the time. *Even after I restore every last inch of this old house, I'm not sure I'll find this place to be a refuge.*

The drumming and pinging in the pots called him back to action. Using the broom as a cane of sorts, he grabbed his baggage and limped back upstairs. The water went into the tub, then he set the pans back in place to catch more.

Russell ventured back into one of the smaller bedrooms. Gritting his teeth against a wave of pain, he leaned against the doorframe and rested a moment. He bent forward, kneaded his thigh to break a cramp, and grunted as he straightened up.

After knocking his way through gargantuan cobwebs, Russell pulled out a dismantled metal bed frame and dragged the parts to his bedchamber where he put the pieces back together. A bedroom door lay across the springs. He sat on it. "Rock hard," he groused. "You'd think they'd have left at least one decent mattress behind."

He'd worn himself out. Russell unrolled both thick wool blankets, used them to form a mattress, then pulled a jacket over himself for a cover. He stared out the window at the rain and realized it was only midafternoon.

Unaccustomed to being unwell, he'd pushed himself all morning in an effort to tamp down any memories or thoughts. Now he'd pay for it. The rest of the day and night stretched ahead, and he had nothing to occupy his hands. Against his will, his mind started heading down the tormenting paths he'd worked so hard to avoid.

&

"Mama, I'm sure someone is up at the big house."

"You said that yesterday, and then the Rimmons' boy came by, looking for their cow."

Lorelei shrugged. "I know."

"So why are you so jumpy? Do you feel we are not safe out here, away from the town?"

"I wouldn't have rented the cottage if I thought we weren't going to be safe, Mama."

Mama bobbed her head in agreement. She sliced cabbage into thin ribbons—some to be coleslaw, the rest to become sauerkraut. She snorted. "Besides, no one would come here to make trouble. That old house is a wreck, and we're too poor to rob."

"The way you're wielding that knife, no one would dare bother us."

"I'd offer them some of my coleslaw and make the enemy my friend, just as the Bible tells me to."

Lorelei shredded carrots. "Where does the Bible talk about coleslaw?"

Mama tried not to smile, but her eyes twinkled. She set down the knife and drummed her fingers on the cutting board. "You shouldn't concern yourself with that. Concentrate on where the Bible talks about children respecting their parents and girls getting married."

Dumping the carrots into the bowl with the cabbage, Lorelei teased, "Mama, don't tell me the Bible mentions South Dakota along with your coleslaw."

Mama pursed her lips and pretended to think on it for a minute. "Remember in Proverbs where it says a meal of herbs in harmony is better than a fatted calf with a contentious wife?"

"I thought we were praying for God to deliver a man to our porch."

"Oh, so that is why you keep thinking you see a man."

Mama's sly look made Lorelei shiver. "Mama, you'd better not be doing anything more than praying. If I find out you've been trying to help God by playing matchmaker, I'm going to be perturbed."

"When have I had a chance to be a matchmaker?" Mama tossed mayonnaise and only a skimpy bit of sugar into the bowl, then started to stir. "Once a week, we go to church. The iceman and the milkman come to make deliveries, but they are both married. I'm going to go to my grave without ever becoming a grandmother."

Lorelei dipped a fork into the bowl, swiped a sample of the coleslaw, and ate it. "Since you're hinting that we have only a matter of hours or days left before God calls us home, I'd go to my grave happy, having tasted your cooking. It's heavenly."

"Heaven should be filled with the sound of children laughing, not the taste of a humble salad."

Though they carried on the conversation as if it were a lark, Lorelei knew her mother was serious. She'd been talking about the future and marriage nonstop ever since Monday's storm. Once Mama got a notion in her mind, it was there to stay. Unwilling to continue the conversation, Lorelei took off her apron and hung it on the hook behind the kitchen door. "It'll be another thirty minutes before the casserole is done cooking. I'll go work on that window a bit more."

"You do that. Be sure to keep your eyes open for that strange man."

"So you do think someone's here!"

Mama shook her head. "No, Lori, I don't." She turned away and added on in a pained voice, "It would be nice to have a man at our table again."

In the months since Papa had left, then after they learned he'd died, Lorelei discovered that Mama would turn to her if she wanted consolation. When Mama spun around the other way, she wanted to be left alone. Respecting her mother's desire for privacy, Lorelei slipped outside.

Lord, this hurts so badly. I miss Papa terribly, and Mama pretends she is okay when I know her heart is broken. Please help us.

four

"Mabel, get on out here." While the storekeeper shouted those words, he kept staring at Russell.

A rawboned woman muttered something under her breath as she came out of the back room. A two-inch brooch secured a red, white, and blue ribbon to her bodice. Russell didn't have to see the picture on the brooch to know it was their son. He braced himself for what he knew would come next.

"We got us a soldier!" The storekeeper came around the counter, headed for Russell, and rubbed his hands in delight. "I can tell by the set of your shoulders—that military bearing is unmistakable."

Russell's stomach started to churn. He hadn't thought to eat before he came, and the emptiness in his belly underscored how little he cared about even the most basic things now. *I just want to buy some stuff and leave.*

The woman shocked Russell when she threw herself at him and hugged him like a long-lost son. "You dear boy! Where were you? Did you meet my Herbert?"

"Herbert Molstead. He's with the First Division." The storekeeper's voice rang with pride. "Eighteenth Infantry Regiment."

Russell awkwardly patted the woman even though he wanted nothing more than to get out of there. "Sorry. I was with the Twenty-eighth."

"Oh." Disappointment creased her face, but she still clung to him.

"Twenty-eighth? That's under Bullard! We got us a whiz-bang hero, Mabel. They beat the socks off the Krauts at Cantigny."

28

The man stood a bit straighter and stuck out his hand. "A pleasure to be in your company, young man."

Still patting the woman with his left hand, Russell reached out and shook hands. "Sir."

"Mabel, turn loose of him and let him tell us all about it."

The last thing Russell wanted to do was talk about the war. These people wanted to hear stories about glory and victory; his memories were gory and vicious. He gently pulled free and indicated the brooch. "What do you hear from Herbert?"

"That boy." Mabel Molstead tsked. "He said he's up to his ankles in mud all of the time."

"Trenches," her husband added knowingly. "Mama's sure he'll catch a cold. She sent him socks."

"I'm sure he'll appreciate them." Russell wanted out of there. He quickly revised his plans. Not wanting to let anyone know he'd taken up residence, he'd ridden to a town just north in order to buy supplies.

On the way here, he'd decided to buy a buckboard so he could haul a mattress back to the estate. Knowing the buckboard would enable him to transport supplies made it a good investment, and the thought of having a comfortable, soft mattress lightened his mood.

Now, those things didn't matter. What he needed most was to get away.

"Oh! Oh, mercy me. You would still be over there unless. . ." Mrs. Molstead's voice died out.

Mr. Molstead cleared his throat. "Yes, well, then. We've been nattering on, and I didn't even ask what you came in to buy."

"Just a few basics." Russell spied a folding cot and reached for it. "Do you have bread, or is there a local bakery?"

Ten minutes—an eternity—later, he secured packs to one horse and mounted up on the other.

"Here, Son. The missus wanted you to have this." Mr. Molstead held up a pair of home-knit socks.

"Much obliged." Russell forced a smile, nodded, and rode off. He'd barely accomplished a thing coming here. No mattress, scant repair materials, and the groceries would last only a few days—especially since he didn't have an icebox. At least he'd gotten parts to repair his pump.

Since his last name was Diamond, the Molsteads wouldn't connect him with the Newcomb family or house. He'd still have his refuge. That and the thought of sleeping on the cot gave Russell grim satisfaction.

❧

"I can see what you mean, Miss Goetz." The sheriff frowned at the big, old house. "Someone's definitely torn down most of the boards. Footprints are fresh, too. I'll go in and take a look-see."

Lorelei nodded. As soon as the sheriff crossed the veranda and stepped foot into the mansion, she scampered up behind him.

"Miss, you'd best not come in here. No telling what I'll find."

"You've taken the county championship for pistol marksmanship for the past three years, Mr. Clem."

His chest puffed out a bit. "Could be whoever's squatting here is outside. Stay close so I know where you are."

"All right." Chills chased down her spine. Lorelei glanced about the entryway.

"Only one fella," the sheriff whispered. "See? One set of boot prints. Dust in here is thick. He's got a bum leg—see how the stride's uneven?"

"Looks like he's gone upstairs a few times." Dust still coated the stairs, but in a very thin layer that bore fresh scuffle marks.

"We'll check downstairs first." Sheriff took his pistol from the holster. "You stay right behind me. Even if he's not here right now, no telling if the floor boards are rotten."

Lorelei felt a spurt of relief that he'd thought of that potential problem. She'd been gawking around from the moment she'd entered and now paid more attention to the floor. She tapped her toe, sending puffs of dust swirling about her worn shoes. "This is marble."

Sheriff started toward the left. "Typical enough of these old houses. Rest of the place ought to be fancy wood floors. No linoleum in the olden days, you know."

"I'd not thought of such a thing." She carefully followed his footsteps through a parlor, then into what must have been a ballroom. The long room at the back of the house where the windows overlooked the ocean held an enormous buffet and a few chairs. "They must have had splendid suppers here."

"Kitchen's likely through these doors." Sheriff Clem cast her a warning look. "The evidence from the outside and the footprints show he's been in there a fair bit. You stay back." A minute later, he called, "It's okay in here."

So far, the rest of the downstairs hadn't been disturbed in ages. Gray-tan dust clung to every surface, giving a dismal air to what once must have been exceptional beauty. She couldn't tell what furniture formed the lumpy shapes under canvas sheets. The sheriff didn't bother to search beneath them because none of the footsteps that stood out in shocking relief on the floors ever approached the abandoned pieces.

Lorelei couldn't believe the difference as she sidled into the kitchen. Clean. The walls, counter, and floor gleamed from a fresh scrubbing. The iron cookstove off to the side was big enough to prepare food for an army. A small hodge-podge of dishes peeked through the glass-fronted doors on one cabinet, and stacks of canned food, neat as a row of soldiers, sat in another.

"Whoever this is, is planning to stay a good long while." The sheriff nosed into the pantry and tilted his head toward another door. "Best be getting on with the search."

An entrance to the other wing hadn't been traversed, so they bypassed it and peeked through the rest of the downstairs, including what had to be one of the most dismal sights Lorelei had ever seen: book-filled shelves in a library, a treasure trove left ignored in the passage of time.

Once upstairs, they discovered the squatter had trundled up and down the hall a few times, but the most noteworthy thing was that he'd scoured the master bedchamber and made it into his own place. A bureau, a table-sized Turkish rug, and a cot showed the mysterious occupant had made an effort to create a tidy, functional place for himself.

"See that cot? Made up right and tight—the military way. We got us a soldier boy here, Miss Goetz. Gotta be careful. Some men go to war and come back tetched in the head. Could be a dangerous situation. I'll see if I can't catch this fella, but until I do, you and your mama might be wise to stay in town."

Lorelei stood in the room and closed her eyes. Sadness swamped her. She opened them and blinked away the tears that threatened. "Whoever this is, he has been here awhile and never bothered us."

"Never know." Sheriff Clem shook his head ponderously and escorted her out of the room. "I reckon you and your mother can ask around to see who'll take you in for a few days until I can come back and lie in wait for this soldier-boy. I've got me some important things to do for the rest of the week. 'Bout middle of next week, I could see my way clear to coming to set a trap for this trespasser."

Her step faltered at the top of the stairs. She stopped and pled, "Must we do anything? Maybe he just needs to rest awhile before he's on his way."

"Trespassing is a crime—and before you let that tender heart of yours come up with excuses, no one had to post signs.

The boards on the doors and windows gave the message loud and clear."

They descended the gritty stairs and went back outside. Sheriff kicked one of the boards that must've once blocked the front door. "Suppose I'd be ten kinds a fool to bother tacking that back up. If he's just resting up, he'd best be gone by next week." His brows beetled, and he gave her a meaningful look.

"I'll talk to Mama and see what she thinks."

He nodded. "You do that, Miss Goetz. It shouldn't take you long to pack a few necessities and walk to town."

The sheriff mounted up and tipped his hat. He rode off down the lawn, across past the shrubs, and took the shortcut to town through the wooded area. For all of his warnings and concerns, he'd not offered to give Lorelei a ride back to her cottage.

She hadn't expected him to. He had two sons in the American Expeditionary Force "over there." Like so many townsfolk, he couldn't quite ignore her last name, accent, or Nordic coloring. He'd done his duty by coming out here to investigate, but the delay in any attempt to apprehend the trespasser because he had "important" things to do made it clear he'd rather wash his hands of the affair.

છ

Russell winced as he exited the narrow passageway. Once he closed the secret door, he limped to the window and braced himself as he watched the man ride off and leave the girl behind.

He'd heard them coming and slipped into the hideaway. Dad had told the story of how the black sheep of the family experienced spiritual revival and had used that passage to get into the house and borrow some keepsakes so he could reproduce them. The missing items caused Great-uncle Duncan to suspect one of the maids was a thief. Once matters were ironed out, Duncan ended up marrying the maid. Aunt Brigit had been one of Dad's favorites. As soon as he had a decent place to sleep, Russell remembered that family lore and had located the secret passageway.

Prying busybodies. They had no call to bother him. He'd kept entirely to himself.

Russell watched as the girl walked the weed-encrusted gravel road that arched around toward the main thoroughfare. She moved gracefully, with a fluid step that made her hem sway. Cutting across the grass would have saved her time and distance. Why would she stay on the path, and why hadn't the sheriff given her a ride back to the cottage? For all of his brave talk about safety, the sheriff had done nothing. He'd left the girl behind, alone.

Pretty thing, too. Tall and willowy. Had sunbeam yellow hair. She halted for a moment, stooped, and rose. Even from her profile, he could see her smile. She held up something and pursed her lips. *Wishing on a dandelion?* "Honey, don't you know wishes and prayers are for children?"

He startled himself by speaking those words aloud. He'd heard everything the sheriff said while they were in the house, but her voice was too soft for Russell to hear most of what she'd said. The lawman called her Miss Gets.

Before enlisting, Russell had worked at his father's emporium. He recognized the material of Miss Gets's dress—one of the economy prints that sold for a paltry three cents per yard three years ago. Money must be tight.

But the sheriff was right—she and her mother shouldn't be living out here alone. Russell knew the caretaker's cottage they inhabited was part of his property. He'd write a letter to his attorney and tell him the place wasn't for rent any longer.

five

"There's definitely someone living up at the big house, Mama." Lorelei tugged the baby blue table oilcloth straight, then put a small vase of pansies in the center.

"It is not our concern. We have no responsibility for that old place."

"I didn't want to worry you, so I went to town and asked the sheriff to meet me there. We went inside."

Mama whirled around from rinsing radishes so quickly, she showered water in an arc around the kitchen. "Lori!"

"It was perfectly safe. You know Sheriff Clem. He even wore his pistol. He walked ahead of me every step of the way."

Mama turned away, banged her hands on the sink to supposedly shake off the water, then came toward the table. The effort she put into wiping her hands off on the dishtowel told Lorelei she was trying to control her temper. "What did you think you were doing, to walk into danger like that? Do not tell me Mr. Clem would protect you. He is one who believed your father went to fight with the Germans. Even after the army delivered those medals saying Johann was a brave American soldier who died for this country, Mr. Clem did not apologize for his ugly lies."

"His wife always talks to us at church."

Mama sighed. "What am I to do with you, Child? You want to believe good of everyone. The world is not like that. It is why Jesus came—because man is sinful. You cannot give away your trust so easily."

"I need to talk with you about that very thing." The chair

scraped the battered linoleum floor as Lorelei pulled it out. She sat down and patted the table in an invitation for Mama to join her.

Mama sat down and folded her hands on the table. Just as quickly as she folded them, she unfolded them and reached out to hold Lorelei's hand. "What is it?"

"Until Sheriff Clem can meet the man who's living at the big house, he thinks we should move back to town. He said it's not safe here for us."

Mama didn't say anything, but her hold tightened.

"I promised him I'd speak with you about it." Lorelei leaned forward. "Mama, I don't want to go back to town. I wouldn't have the workshop, and it's important for me to honor my promises to complete the windows on time."

"Your safety is more important than a thousand windows."

"I feel that way about you, too, Mama." She shrugged. "I don't feel scared at all out here. Even when I was in the mansion, I didn't worry."

"Tell me then why the sheriff thinks we are unsafe here."

"From what we saw, only one man is there. Mama, he's probably a soldier. Sheriff Clem judged the footprints to be made by a lame man. More than that. . ." She paused and tapped her temple. "The sheriff thinks he could be dangerous because war can change men."

"This is true. It can." Mama ran her forefinger down Lorelei's arm. "You have been thinking. I can see it in your eyes."

"I have." Lorelei leaned forward. "Mama, if Papa had come home from war with an injury, we wouldn't love him any less."

"Of course not."

"I was thinking, if the injury wasn't a physical one—if his mind or spirit was hurt—we would still love him."

"So you are thinking this soldier man hiding in that old house might bear an unseen wound. Though the sheriff's warning seems prudent, your heart tells you otherwise."

Lorelei smiled. "Oh, Mama, I was hoping you'd understand."

"This isn't something you decide without prayer. While you make sandwiches, I'll read the Bible. We can pray and talk about it during lunch."

Papa always read the Bible and said family prayers at the close of supper. When he shipped overseas, Mama reasoned that France was six hours ahead of Virginia, so if they had their devotions at lunch, it would be at the same time Papa was. That way, they'd all read the same chapters and worship together as a family.

Mama started reading from the second chapter of Nehemiah:

> *"Wherefore the king said unto me, Why is thy countenance sad, seeing thou art not sick? this is nothing else but sorrow of heart. . .then I was very sore afraid, And said unto the king, Let the king live for ever: why should not my countenance be sad, when the city, the place of my fathers' sepulchres, lieth waste, and the gates thereof are consumed with fire? Then the king said unto me, For what dost thou make request? So I prayed to the God of heaven. And I said unto the king, If it please the king, and if thy servant have found favour in thy sight, that thou wouldest send me unto Judah, unto the city of my fathers' sepulchres, that I may build it."*

Lorelei drew in a deep breath and let it out slowly. "Mama, those verses—they never really meant anything to me before. This time, they jump out. If this man has a sorrow of the heart, I want to help."

Resting her hand on the thin pages of the open Bible, Mama fell silent.

Lorelei wanted to plead her case. The verses spoke so clearly to her of a man who had suffered and needed to find a safe home again. Still, the decision wasn't hers to make—at least, not alone. Whatever they did, Mama needed to feel at peace, too. Mind racing, Lorelei thought of things she could say that might convince her mother to agree to befriend the stranger. Failing that, she thought of people in town Mama might stay with if she felt scared.

The knife cut through the bread at a slant, creating uneven slices that told of her impatience. Mayonnaise. Lettuce and tomatoes fresh from the garden. Some salami. It took only seconds to make lunch, but in that time, Lorelei prepared an argument worthy of being heard by the Supreme Court. She turned back to her mother.

"Don't," Mama said softly. "I know what you want, Lori, but this is not about what we want; it is about what God would have us do."

Lorelei let out a guilty laugh. "You're right. Still, Mama, there can't be anything wrong with leaving a little food for him."

"How do you know he's hungry?"

"There hasn't been any smoke from the chimney or stovepipe."

"So you are imagining this soldier is going without his daily bread?" Mama shook her head. "Lorelei, if you feed him, you encourage him to stay."

"He's not a stray cat!" Lorelei set the plates on the table and let out a short laugh. "It's too bad he's not. Have you seen how many field mice we've had around here?"

"Deer, rabbits, gophers. . ." Mama gazed out the window. "They're going to eat up half of my garden."

"He's living up there and hasn't stolen a single thing from the garden, Mama. Did you notice? It would have been so easy for him to help himself—especially at night."

"If you weren't so talented at making such beautiful windows, I would say your time is wasted here and you should stay in town and sell things. You could make a poor man buy a wallet!"

Lorelei laughed guiltily. "Okay. So let's pray and eat."

They stretched their hands across the table to meet in the middle. Mama's hands felt cool, slightly rough, and reassuring. Even so, Lorelei missed Papa's big, strong hands turning their grasp into a triangle.

"Heiliger Vater in Himmel," Mama began. She always prayed in German.

Holy Father in heaven. The rest of the prayer poured forth, but Lorelei clung to the very first words. War robbed her of her beloved earthly father, but he'd taught her to rely on her heavenly Father—and that brought solace in times like this.

୬

Russell froze as he heard footsteps on the veranda. They were tentative. *Because someone is sneaking up on me? No. The weight is too slight, the shoes heeled. If the woman is scared, why would she bother to come here?*

He heard her next few steps, and realization dawned. She tested each step she took before putting her full weight on it—wisely checking to see if the rotting boards were safe. The footsteps finally stopped, only to be replaced with three uncertain knocks on the door.

He'd hoped the sheriff's warning would be sufficient. Clearly, someone ignored it and decided to get snoopy. Folks were like that, but Russell didn't want to be around anyone. He refused to go answer the door. He stood stock-still and waited until he heard the woman leave the veranda. A wry smile twisted his mouth. She made faster time on her retreat. More likely, she was scared of him rather than it simply being a matter of her retracing her steps so she'd use the boards she knew to be safe.

He quietly crossed the parlor and drew back the very edge of the heavy draperies. From that vantage point, he could see the lissome blond sauntering back down the road. Her flour sack dress swayed with each step, swishing gently from side to side in a uniquely feminine way. Odd, how many little things he'd forgotten while living in the muddy trenches with men.

About twenty feet from the house, she turned around and gave a fleeting look at the porch. A smile chased across her face, then she looked up at the upstairs windows. Her smile faltered, but Russell felt a stab of relief that she didn't sense where he stood. He didn't want any connection to anyone.

"Go home, Buttercup," he whispered. "You don't belong here."

As if she heard him, she whirled around and walked out of sight.

He'd been going from room to room, trying to decide which projects needed immediate attention and what could wait. He'd been up on the roof. The whole thing needed to be stripped down to the base and completely reboarded and reshingled. Russell couldn't haul the wood up and do the work alone, and he didn't want to have to deal with others, which led him to the dismaying conclusion that he'd need to hire others to come do the task.

While in town, he'd go ahead and purchase supplies for several other repairs. In fact, he'd buy a buckboard. By loading it high, Russell reckoned he'd be able to stock up on enough that he'd be able to avoid making several trips.

Last night, as he fell asleep, he'd already made a mental list of half-a-dozen items he needed. Upon awakening and walking around, he'd added to that list until he needed to actually write down everything. Tomorrow or the next day, he'd grit his teeth and ride in.

For now, he'd leave the parlor and library as they stood. Due to the way the wind blew off the ocean and their intact windows, those two rooms had the least amount of grime in them. Russell took a quick peek under the heavy sailcloth at an ornate set of nesting tables. Once the rest of the room was restored, these would make a nice addition to the furniture.

Then again, so little furniture remained, he'd have to be satisfied with what was on hand unless he went to town to shop for more or made it himself.

Russell chewed on the tip of the pencil, then scrawled on the paper, "boards for porch." He couldn't risk someone falling through the disintegrating planks. Maybe he hadn't wanted to do that as a first project, but given the curiosity factor of his neighbor and the sheriff, he didn't have much choice.

In the meantime, he'd go ahead and shore up the existing porch for safety's sake. A fistful of nails, his hammer, and the boards he'd ripped from the windows would do the trick. Russell opened the front door and stopped cold.

A small basket sat there, a rust-colored gingham cloth covering its contents.

Russell wanted to ignore it. If he accepted a neighbor's gift, he'd end up having to interact and be sociable. The thought curdled his stomach. He stepped over the basket and avoided looking at it again as he assessed the planks. As he scanned the boards and visually measured their lengths and condition, the basket kept coming back in view.

Seeing it was bad enough; smelling it was worse. The aroma of fresh-baked bread sneaked past the cloth covering and tempted him to eat his fill. Russell swallowed and turned away. One nail. Two. Three. He banged each in place and lied to himself with each of them. *I don't want bread. I don't. Not a bite.*

He sat back on his heels and studied the porch a bit more. *The first week I was in Buttonhole, your mama stopped by with a big old basket with cornbread, chicken stew, jam, and applesauce.* His father told that story often enough. Mama was famous for her baskets. Russell grew up watching her cook far too much, then slip extra loaves of bread, jars of soup, jam, vegetables, and cookies into her baskets and set out to deliver them to whomever she fancied might need them.

"I'm not a charity case." He punctuated his rough words with a few bangs of the hammer. The basket jumped.

Try as he might, he couldn't ignore the aroma. Russell argued with himself, hated his weakness, but still leaned back, snatched the wicker handle, and yanked the basket onto his thighs. He swept off the rusty, checkered napkin and inhaled. Several slices of bread, a pint jar of jam, an earthenware crock of baked beans, another of coleslaw, and a savory, two-inch-round length of bratwurst filled the basket to overflowing.

His lap was full, but his heart and stomach ached with emptiness. Russell stared at the offering. When he saw the neatly printed label on the jar of jam, he lost the battle. Peach jam. How many hundreds of jars of peach jam had Mama cooked and delivered? She'd done so in her special way—with that gentleness of wanting to be kind to another. The young woman—Buttercup—had done the selfsame thing. That fact slipped past his defenses.

Russell scooted backward until his spine rested against the house, unscrewed the lid, and dipped his finger into the jam.

୨ଈ

Russell waited until night fell. He'd kept busy all day, then washed up. Round about midnight, he slipped out of the mansion and approached the small cottage on the edge of the property. At least two hours had passed since the lamps in the cottage went out, so he felt certain the women were fast asleep.

He knew two women lived there. The laundry on the line broadcast that fact. He'd also been spying from his attic window. Buttercup lived there—probably with her mother, from the looks of things. A pathetically small woodpile slumped along the back fence, one of the two chimneys lacked a few bricks at the top, and the place needed basic repairs.

Carefully, quietly, Russell walked from his home to the cottage with his arms full. He stacked several logs onto their woodpile and carried a few more to their back porch. He wouldn't need all that much for himself, and he'd have all summer and autumn to chop more. It was the least he could do as repayment for the food they'd given.

By returning the basket and dishes and leaving wood, he turned their charity into a barter. Satisfied with that arrangement, he turned to go home.

A small whimper stopped him in his tracks.

six

"Poor girl," he said as he approached the small form. Fifteen minutes later, Russell carefully peeled his shirt from around the mutt and gently petted her between the ears. Glad he'd cleaned out the stovepipes the day before, Russell started a fire in the stove to provide some radiant heat for the dog and boil water to cleanse her wounds.

The poor beast looked like she'd been struck by a motorcar. One hind leg and her tail were injured—just how seriously, Russell couldn't tell. The dog seemed to sense Russell meant to help her. She weakly licked his hand as he finished bathing away the dirt and blood. After dipping a white cotton dishcloth into the boiling water several times, Russell tore it into strips and used them as bandages. It wasn't until he finished that he let out a rueful laugh.

"You're going to have a limp just like me. Same leg, even. We're a sad pair."

The dog yawned and rested her muzzle on his thigh. Russell stroked her ears. "I guess I'm stuck with you."

⁂

Sunday morning, Lorelei left a basket on the porch of the big house and scurried back down the road. She and Mama needed to hurry so they wouldn't be late for church. This was the third basket she'd left for the strange soldier.

Both times she'd left baskets, he'd returned them along with doing a chore as payment. They now had plenty of firewood and the well sported a new rope and bucket. Lorelei didn't want him to think he had to barter for the food they gave, but it was nice to have someone see to the details that slipped her notice or strained her abilities.

Mama came out of the cottage and tucked a hanky into her purse. "Hurry. We don't want to be late for church."

"We'll be on time."

Mama wrinkled her nose. "I want to be there a little bit early. It's past time for Sheriff Clem to tell us what he's found out about the man up at the house."

"He hasn't bothered to do anything more, Mama."

"Unless he benefits, the sheriff lets matters slide." Mama fell into step with her. "He claims to be busy, but most afternoons, he either sits at the counter at Phoebe's, drinking free coffee, or he goes off to play poker at David McGee's."

Lorelei laughed. "I suppose we ought to be glad he's coming to church. Perhaps his heart will be touched."

"Maybe we can ask Mr. Rawlin about the house." Mama walked around one side of a mud puddle while Lorelei went around the other. "He's in charge of the property. When we wanted to rent the cottage, we had to work with him."

Lorelei nodded. Mr. Rawlin had taken care of the matter—even though she'd suspected he didn't want to lease to them. "Maybe he could rent the place to the soldier. It would be a fair trade if he could stay there for all of the cleaning and repairs he's doing."

Mama stopped. A stricken look chased across her face. "We ought to have invited him to come to worship with us."

"I did, Mama. I slipped a note in with the basket on Friday."

❧

"I'll be back soon." Russell petted the dog as he spoke. She'd lapped up half of the can of beef broth. "They've gone off to church, so I'll slip down to the cottage. I'll be back before you know it."

The unbandaged tip of her tail wagged weakly on the

kitchen floor. Russell didn't know exactly what to do for her, but he'd applied the first aid he'd been taught and hoped it would be enough to let the dog heal.

Russell wanted the women to leave for church, and he'd hoped it would be late enough in the morning that the ground would have dried from any dew. Ever since he'd returned home, Russell couldn't stomach the smell of morning-damp earth. Rain didn't bother him: it carried a sweetness to it that helped. But he'd spent too many frigid predawn hours in the trenches with the loamy smell of dirt overpowering him.

He stepped outside and breathed through his mouth to minimize his sense of smell. *Okay. It's okay.* He let out a sigh of relief, then hefted a few scrap lengths of planking over his shoulder and grabbed a small crate containing nails, a hammer, folding measuring stick, pencil, and saw. On the way to the cottage, he managed to stumble twice due to his weak leg. Anger welled up. Though no one witnessed his awkwardness, Russell still hated it and all it brought back. He went to the front of the cottage and dumped the boards with a satisfying clatter.

Then he saw it: the flag in the front window. The background was white, just like the draperies, which is why he hadn't seen it from far off. In the center was a star—but not the blue one that proclaimed the family had a son, brother, or father at war. This one featured a gold star carefully stitched over that blue one—a heartbreaking testament that their man wouldn't be coming home.

Russell stood and stared at the flag. Fury welled up. He took another look at the small porch and went into a frenzy, completely shattering the warped boards and dismantling the entire structure. As soon as he pried the last board free, he stared at the mess he'd created. What was supposed to have been a few simple replacement boards resulted in this galling destruction. He'd been enraged at the loss these women suffered, but his actions only caused more problems. He let out a long, deep sigh.

He couldn't very well go into town on Sunday and buy boards, but tomorrow, he'd be able to get the lumber to do the job. Then again, he didn't dare leave the porch as it was. He searched about for wood.

A stack of storm windows lay on the leeward side of a fair-sized workshop. Russell selected those with the sturdiest wood and carried them to the front door. By setting them in place, he created a temporary walkway. Anxious to leave before they returned from church, he left a note under the front door.

❧

"Miss Goetz, I need to speak with you for a moment." Mr. Rawlin looked at her steadily as his wife bustled away to claim their youngsters from Sunday school.

"Oh, good." She slipped out of the pew, into the aisle. Mr. Rawlin invariably discussed matters out of earshot. She figured as an attorney, he had to guard his tongue and weigh his words more carefully. That being the case, she waited to mention anything about the stranger staying at the house until they got outside.

"The sheriff mentioned someone's living up at the big house," Mr. Rawlin said.

"Yes. He's fixing things up and cleaning."

The attorney nodded sagely. "Makes perfect sense. He's undoubtedly the new owner. The old one died, and I contacted his heir—a great-nephew." He smoothed his tie. "He's a good man—a war hero. I'm sure you and your mother will be safe."

"Thank you. He hasn't troubled us at all."

❧

He hasn't troubled us at all. Lorelei's words echoed back in her shocked mind as she stared in horror at the porch when she and Mama got home. *I spoke too soon.*

"Mercy, mercy!" Mama blotted her forehead with her hanky. "Will you look at that!"

"I am." The two words caught in her throat and came out in a strangled croak.

"That just proves it."

Lorelei bowed her head in defeat. She and Mama would have to find somewhere else to live—but where?

"God provides our every need," Mama smiled. "That old porch—you are slender, and it doesn't mind you, but it's started to creak and groan under my feet. I was nervous to use the front door anymore." Nimble as a mountain goat, she climbed the three makeshift steps, crossed the storm window "porch," and opened the front door.

"Mama, be careful."

Mama turned around. Her eyes twinkled—a rare event these days. "You're too late to say that, Lori. Come, now. Oh, look! We have a message here."

Lorelei joined her mother in a flash. On the back of a long list of tools and supplies, in a bold scrawl done in pencil, he'd written, "Wood was rotting and dangerous. Be careful. Will finish soon."

"Isn't that nice of him?"

"Yes, is it, Mama."

"What a pity that he didn't come to church, though."

20

It was too late by the time he spotted her. Busy thinking about what more he could do for Mutt, Russell hadn't paid attention. Monday morning, he went out the front door and nearly knocked over the girl. "Whoa!" He instinctively grabbed her arms to keep her from tumbling backward.

She let out a gasp, then got her footing. Color flooded her cheeks even though he released her. "Excuse me. I brought you this." She nudged the basket into his arms and stepped back.

"Your list. . .tools and wood and things. . ." She nervously moistened her lips. "I thought you might want it back."

He nodded curtly.

"I—I heard a woofing sound when I came the other day. There is a bone for your dog."

His chin came up. *She's been spying on me.*

"Thank you for the firewood and the porch." She'd inched back toward the steps, and the morning sun glinted on her pale hair and a necklace—a very plain, rather small, silver cross. "It is very kind of you to help us, Sir." He gave no reply, so she whispered, "Good-bye."

As she walked off, Russell stared at her back and felt a bolt of hatred nearly consume him. *She's German.*

seven

As he rode down the path toward town, Russell cast a quick look at the cottage. He'd given his word that he'd repair the porch, and he'd honor it. Then again, he owned the property. He didn't want anyone living there—especially not the enemy. He sought out the lawyer's shingle as he rode down Main Street.

"Mr. Diamond." The attorney reached out to shake hands.

Russell automatically scanned to be sure Mr. Rawlin didn't have a knife or pistol in his other hand. The notion was ludicrous, but life in the trenches taught a man to be cautious. Satisfied no danger existed, Russell shook hands and refused the proffered seat.

"What can I help you with?"

"I don't want anyone on my property. Get rid of the renters."

Mr. Rawlin slowly eased back to lean against his big mahogany desk. "I'm afraid that's not possible. Your great-uncle signed a ten-year lease with the Goetz women."

"Ten years!"

Drumming his fingers on the desktop on either side of his hips, the attorney nodded. "It was old Timothy Newcomb's idea. I confess, I tried to talk him out of it. Stubborn old man wouldn't be swayed. He wanted to be sure the women would have a safe haven. I suppose by now you've determined they are of German heritage."

Russell folded his arms across his chest.

Mr. Rawlin heaved a sigh. "I confess, at the start, I wasn't any happier about it than you are."

"Then find a way to break the deal."

The attorney shook his head. "Johann Goetz gave his life for this country. Last year, when the War Board started gearing up for us to enter the Great War, they knew they'd need reliable men who spoke German. Being close to D.C. as we are, they had a few scouts come out and nose around. Johann was a shade older than they wanted—thirty-nine—but they needed him, and he went."

Russell didn't move an inch or say a word.

"Gossips whispered plenty. Your great-uncle always had the *Gazette* mailed to him. It's featured several articles about the vandalism against Germans in this area. Just north of here, a German was lynched, and the jury found the men who did it innocent. In that same edition, a letter to the editor hinted that Mr. Goetz went off to fight with the Jerries." He paused. When Russell said nothing, the lawyer continued, "Just about that time, Lorelei came to me and asked to rent the cottage. I didn't want to, but as a professional I had to set aside my own feelings and serve my client. I contacted him, and he gave me instructions."

"A decade was extreme." Russell scowled at him.

"I thought so, too, but that's what your uncle specified. He was worried someone might take a mind to smash up her place like they have others."

"From the looks of things, no one bothers them at all."

"Perhaps because they moved out of town. Problems happen—especially here along the coast where folks have lost their sons at sea even before we got sucked into the war."

Russell had heard of such events. He thought of the star flag in the cottage window. *But anyone could put that up. It doesn't actually prove their man was fighting with the Americans.*

"Most of the gossip stopped when posthumous awards arrived for Mr. Goetz," Rawlin continued. "Your uncle figured it's been hard on those women and that they deserved better."

The star stitched on the flag in the window was gold. Russell couldn't argue with what he'd been told. If anything, he owed that widow and her daughter some help—it was a soldier's duty to see to a fallen comrade's families.

"The bank is expecting you to come by and put your signature on file." Clearly, the attorney chose not to press the issue of his renters any further. "The inheritance is in your name, and you can draw on it as you see fit." He glanced down at the papers in front of himself and read off the latest bank balance.

Russell stared at the papers in shock. *Dad told me I'd have enough to live on. He didn't tell me I'd be rich. Ten men couldn't squander that much money in their lifetimes.*

"I took the liberty of opening an account for you at Sander's Mercantile so you can get supplies. Did you require anything else?"

"No." Russell started to walk out. He stopped at the door and turned. "The house needs to be re-roofed immediately. Do you recommend anyone?"

"Want it done cheap, or want it done right?"

"Right." Even if he hadn't inherited a fortune, he would have given that answer, but the fact that the lawyer even bothered to ask the question seemed bizarre.

Rawlin jerked his thumb toward the north. "Pinkus Bayley. Gray house with the red shutters. Don't let his age fool you. He used to be a shipwright. He can gather the best men in short order. Let him buy the supplies—he'll get a better deal."

"Thanks."

The livery had hitches for his team and a sound-looking buckboard. The man in charge sat on a stool, showing a couple of strapping teens how to splice rope. "Don't suppose you got any work out there at your place, do you?" one of the youngsters asked.

"My boys are hard workers," the livery owner added.

Russell didn't want people all over his place. Then again, he'd have the crew doing the roofing. *I might as well get it all over at once and be done with it.* "My stable's a wreck. Needs a thorough cleaning."

The younger lad's voice cracked and went up several notes. "We're used to mucking out stables. You came to the right place to hire yourself some workers."

"Show up tomorrow—two hours after daybreak. I'll pay you two bucks a day apiece." Russell watched how their eyes lit up. "For that kind of money, I expect you to be men—not boys who need directions."

"We can do it!"

"Fine. I've got things to see to here in town. My horses could stand for some decent feed—corn and oats. I'll be about two hours, so take care of them now, then have them hitched and ready to go."

At the feed store, Russell arranged for corn, oats, and hay to be delivered at the end of the week. By then, the stable would be ready to hold the supplies.

Next, Russell stopped by the post office and mailed a letter to his mother. He'd taken pains to write more than the fact that he'd arrived at the mansion. After two paragraphs, he'd included as much as he could concoct, then signed, "Love, Russell." It wouldn't win a prize, but it fulfilled his promise. He hoped, it would settle Mama's fears.

By the time he reached the diner, Russell's leg ached abominably. He slid into a seat and ignored the assessing looks of others by staring sightlessly at the menu. It would be like every other menu nowadays—featuring so-called patriotic dishes like victory burgers and liberty cabbage, and a reminder about meatless Mondays and wheatless Wednesdays.

"Have you decided what you want?"

"I'll have the blue plate special," he ordered without glancing up. In an attempt to keep from having to strike up a conversation, he pulled the list from his pocket and reviewed it. When the waitress slid a plate of liver and onions in front of him, he winced.

A brawny, middle-aged man swaggered up, grabbed the plate, and shoved it back at the waitress. "That's not fit for eatin'. Give him meat and 'taters. Bring me a steak while you're at it." He slid into the seat opposite Russell and leaned back with more show than a rodeo pony. "Chester Gimley. Figured you'd be lookin' to have someone do the work out at that old place. I can do anything you want. Cheap."

"And I reckon," the waitress said as she thumped the plate back down in front of Russell, "Mr. Diamond can eat anything he orders. In case you didn't notice, he's concentrating on his work."

"Mind your own business, Myrtle."

"Gimley?" Russell looked at him, and the stranger's eyes brightened with greed. "I don't hold with a man treating a woman with disrespect."

Gimley went ruddy and blustered, but he didn't apologize.

Russell deliberately picked up his knife and fork and cut into the revolting slab of liver. He took a big bite, promptly washed it down with his coffee, and realized it didn't taste any better or worse than anything else he'd had in weeks. He ate because he needed to, but everything got stuck halfway down and had to be washed past the ever-present ball in his throat.

Gimley snorted derisively, shoved away from the table, and stomped off.

Half an hour later, Russell left the diner with his stomach churning. He stopped at the gray house with the red shutters, struck a deal with old Pinkus Bayley to replace the roof, and gladly accepted a glass of bicarbonate before he left.

The mercantile made him suffer a momentary pang of homesickness. Dad's emporium carried the same wondrous mixture of aromas—briny pickles, sweet, fresh fruit, the tang of new leather goods, and the honest scent of soap. Drawing the list from his pocket, Russell started searching for the items. In a matter of minutes, Mr. Sanders and his daughter, Olivia, were both helping him. It didn't take long before his order filled the entire counter and formed an appreciable heap on the floor.

Staples, eggs, produce, three one-pound cans of coffee, and a crate overflowing with cans and jars of food sat next to a frying pan, cast iron pots, and a kettle.

"Looks like you're feeding an army," Mr. Saunders teased.

Russell ignored the comment and added molasses to the supplies. The beans Buttercup brought in the first basket had been sweetened a tad with molasses, and he'd had a hankering for more. *I can make them for myself. I don't want her cooking for me.*

"I have just the thing for you: Kirby's Ezee 'Grasshopper' vacuum cleaner." Olivia demonstrated it and added, "It requires no electricity."

Russell hastily propped it against the icebox. Doing so knocked the Johnson's prepared wax for the floor from atop the stack and created quite a ruckus.

Russell startled at the sound and broke out in a cold sweat. For a few horrible moments, he was in the trenches again, hearing the clatter of equipment. His heart raced, and he kept clutching his fists as he reminded himself that he didn't need to grab his rifle or knife. Everything within him screamed to retreat, yet Miss Olivia stood there giggling behind her hand while her father unrolled a mattress for his inspection.

The mattress. I need the mattress. I have to get this stuff so I can stay home and not come back for a long time. Russell snatched the dipper from the water bucket and gulped several mouthfuls, then croaked, "The mattress is fine. I'll take it."

Folks in the store chattered just like they did back in Dad's place. Russell knew it was all just neighborly talk—snoopy, helpful, good-natured. Nonetheless, he was on edge. He'd turned down at least half-a-dozen housekeeping offers and didn't care what they thought his total bill would come to.

". . .sheets, a pillow, and blankets?"

Russell realized Mr. Saunders had asked him a question. He nodded and rasped, "Add it all up and put it on my account. I'll go fetch my buckboard." He got out of there as fast as he could limp.

❧

Lorelei hoed the garden and watched the road. He'd taken both horses and headed toward town. She wanted to ask her neighbor a favor, and it had taken her hours to build up her courage after he'd scared her this morning. She heard the trundling sound of a wagon and the jingle of harnesses before he came into view.

As she wiped her hands on a rag, Lorelei went to stand in the middle of the road. Mr. Diamond looked about as cheerful as a thundercloud when he pulled the team to a stop.

"Mr. Diamond, I have a favor I'd like to ask of you." When he made no reply, Lorelei wrapped her arms about her waist and forged on. *Nothing ventured, nothing gained.* "Mama and I garden. We've planted a Victory Garden—like they have in England—and many folks in town buy our produce. I wanted to ask you to let me sharecrop a tiny section of your land."

"I'll think about it."

His reply surprised her. She'd braced herself for a flat refusal and dared to hope for agreement. Never once had she thought he might delay making a decision. Lorelei blinked at him for a moment, then tucked a wind-whipped strand of hair behind her ear. "Thank you."

He stared off to the side. His eyes carried a haunted look, and the set of his jaw didn't invite further conversation. In fact, the raspy quality to his voice made it sound as if he rarely spoke.

Lorelei sidled off the path and watched as he nickered and the handsome pair of geldings set the buckboard in motion. She'd wanted to intercept him without Mama overhearing the request. Worried as she was about money, Mama would get her hopes up or be in a dither that the neighbor would deduce their finances were strained. This way, Mama wouldn't know a thing if he refused them.

Lorelei went back to the garden and picked up the hoe. She carried it to a small shed, then washed up at the pump and went back to the workshop.

Mama was sweeping the workroom floor. Lorelei stooped, held the dustpan, and smiled at the tinkling sound as all of the tiny bits hit the thin steel. "In my fanciful moments, I imagine that's what the angels' laughter sounds like."

Mama smoothed her hair. "Ah, my Lori. It takes so little to make you happy."

"You're the one who taught me to count my blessings." She rose and dumped the sweepings into the wastebasket as she began to sing:

> Count your blessings, name them one by one;
>> Count your blessings, see what God hath done;
> Count your blessings, name them one by one;
>> Count your many blessings, see what God hath done.

Mama had joined in on the last two lines. Afterward, she brushed away a tear. *"Du bist mein Segen, Lorelei."*

"You're my blessing, too, Mama."

"It would be nice to have the blessing of more orders." Mama fiddled with the last remaining order slip on the board.

"Papa always said, 'God will provide.' He'd want us to have faith."

"Yes, he would." Mama tugged a hanky out of her sleeve and wiped her cheeks. "I will take some lettuce and cabbage into town tomorrow. It will buy more flour for us."

"See? God provides."

◆

Sleep didn't come easily or well for Russell. Even on his new mattress, he'd jerk awake and reach for his rifle. He'd rolled out of bed before dawn and made a pot of coffee. As he finished the last sip, wagons rolled up.

I told them not to come until two hours after daybreak. Irritated, Russell thumped down his empty mug and went outside.

"She's a beauty," Pinkus Bayley said as he admired the old house. "We'll have her looking grand as can be in no time at all."

"Warn your men that the veranda is rotting in places and they'll need to test their footing. I don't want anyone breaking a leg."

"Hear that, men?" Pinkus clapped his hands and rubbed them together. Russell estimated it was more out of eagerness to begin than from a need to warm them. "Even from here, I can see you're right. We'll take it clear down to the joists and put up all new slats, felt, tar paper, and shingles."

"I'll set a water bucket and dipper here for the men."

"Jim-dandy idea." Pinkus turned back to his men. "Daniel, go check out the chimneys to be sure they're sound. Jake and Ed, I want you to scythe the grass over yonder. We'll dump the old shingles and rotten wood there. We'll have us a bonfire when the job's finished."

The liveryman's sons rode up together on a swaybacked mare. *Can't anyone in this town follow directions or tell time?* Russell took them over to the stable and pulled open one of the creaky, weathered doors.

"We'll oil the hinges, Mr. Diamond," the elder boy said as he put his weight behind the companion door and got it to budge. "Pa said we need to be sure to wash down everything after we clean it out. No putting your team in here until then, else they'll like to take sick."

Russell frowned at the boys' worn shoes. "Might be snakes in here. I'm sure every last spider in Virginia is. Go on back to town and tell Mr. Sanders to put you in boots."

The boys exchanged a worried look.

"A man pays for the tools and equipment for jobs on his place. Boots—sturdy boots—are a necessity. He's to put them on my account."

"Pa don't cotton to folks takin' charity."

Russell gave the boys a steely-eyed look. "I don't cotton to someone else giving orders to my hired help. While you're here, you'll do as I say."

"Yessir."

Russell headed back toward the house. The work there literally started with a crash bang. Shingles and boards slid off the roof and smashed onto the earth. Pinkus jerked his chin toward Russell.

"Yeah?"

"Most of the chimneys are in fair condition. The mortar needs some patching, but that's not much. The one to the parlor needs to be torn down at least to the bottom floor and rebuilt. It's about to topple. I'll need to be getting sand and gravel to make cement and a load of bricks. Daniel's best as they come on chimneys. After we're done, he'll clean 'em all. Until then, don't set any fires."

"Okay." Russell squinted toward the cottage. *It's my property, and I'm responsible for it.* "Have Daniel repair and clean the chimney over at the caretaker's cottage while he's out here."

"Aye. Fine notion. My men brought lunch buckets today,

but most often, folks feed them when they work. Mrs. Goetz is a dandy cook. Think you can talk her into setting up our dinners?"

"We'll see." Russell looked back at the top of his house. The smallest effort made shingles come loose and skid. Much to his relief, all of the men were wearing safety ropes.

Pinkus cupped his gnarled hands and shouted, "Ed! Wind and rain pattern would hit the southeast corner hardest. I expect the boards there are weak. Don't go over there. You've eaten too many of your wife's noodles!"

The men chuckled, and Russell knew he'd gotten the right man for the job.

Pinkus slanted him a sly look. "I know what you're thinking. I'm older than dirt. Seventy-one. Fought in the War Between the States."

Russell didn't reply to that revelation, though it surprised him.

"When I got home, I didn't want to talk to a soul." Pinkus squinted at the roof and rubbed his chin. "I reckon folks are makin' pests of themselves. I told my men they're to concentrate on this job, not on whatever's happening 'over there.' ?"

Russell froze. The old man's insight stunned him.

"I'm glad you're takin' care of the Goetz women. Things are tight for them 'specially since they lost Johann. Admirable Christians, staunch Americans. You gonna have little Lorelei replace your broken windows?"

"Windows?"

"She took on her father's trade. Good at it, too. A dab hand at glazing windows and puts together some mighty fine stained-glass church windows. From the looks of it, you have plenty of cracked and broken panes."

"One thing at a time." Russell didn't want to have anyone here at all—let alone a woman. A pretty woman.

One who was German.

They parted, and Pinkus went to holler orders to his men as Russell trudged toward the caretaker's cottage. He started toward the front door, then recalled he'd torn the porch to shreds. As he knocked on the back door, he secretly hoped no one would be home.

eight

Pale blue, striped curtains with cherries dotting them parted. Buttercup—*Lorelei,* he corrected himself since he'd learned her name from Pinkus—peeked out. She smiled and opened the door.

"Why, hello."

"Is your mother here?"

"No, she went to town today. Can I help you?"

Russell shifted his weight from both feet onto just the left. His right leg ached. "I need to speak with her."

"She should be home later." She bit her lip for a second. "Is something wrong?"

"No." He hated to have to ask for help. Waiting only meant he'd have to come back. "I'm going to need dinner for the workmen each day. 'Round about noon—something good and filling. Counting the boys cleaning out the stable, there are ten of us. Do you think your mother could cook?"

"Yes. Yes! Mama loves to cook. We have a wagon. I can help her pull the food up to the house."

"You can't very well walk into town and drag back the rest of what you'll need in a kids' wagon. Can you drive a buckboard?"

Her eyes sparkled as she nodded.

"Do you have an ice box?"

"Yes. Ice is delivered every Thursday."

"We won't need food today. Starting tomorrow at noon, I want solid meals. No skimping. I'll give your mother a note for the butcher and the mercantile so she can get whatever she needs." At that moment, Russell realized the mercantile wouldn't be a problem, but the butcher might well be ugly about selling meat to a German. He added on, "I'll make it clear she's my cook and feeding my workmen, so there shouldn't be a problem with her buying the necessary bulk."

Lorelei smiled. "It will be a lot of food. How many days will they be working?"

"Two weeks." Her question took him by surprise. He'd expected her to ask how much he'd pay. "New York house-maids earn eighteen dollars a week." He'd decided twenty would be fair, but Pinkus's words echoed in his mind. *Things are tight. Lost Johann. . .* A closer look showed Lorelei's dress and shoes were both nearly worn out.

"Eighteen dollars!" Her eyes grew huge. "But that is New York."

"I'm sure cooks make far more, and I'm asking your mother to feed several hungry men, even if it's only one meal a day. Tell her I'll pay thirty a week on top of whatever the food costs."

He spun around and made it down the steps before she stammered, "Do you have dishes and tableware enough for ten men at your house?"

Dishes and tableware enough, he repeated to himself. *It's not just her voice that sounds German. She puts the words together wrong.*

"We have dishes if you don't." She spoke the words softly, tentatively.

Russell thought of the mismatched left-behinds he'd gath-ered. He didn't own enough to have one guest at his table, let alone nearly a dozen. The notion of doing any formal enter-taining left him cold, but he refused to depend on someone else for anything as basic as table service. "Get dishes. None of those painted steel things—real ones."

"Fancy china?"

Having worked at Diamond Emporium and ordered stock through catalogues, he knew far more than most men ever would concerning domestic goods. He could handle this. Relieved to be dealing with something straightforward and unemotional, Russell turned.

"Haviland. They have an everyday pattern called Ranson that will do. If that's not available, get Spode's Tower."

"Ranson," she repeated in a tone that matched her astonished expression. She leaned into the doorsill. "What about glasses and such?"

"A case of whatever pressed glass they have on hand. I'll probably use most of the glasses to mix paint or clean brushes. When the house was locked up, they left a mishmash of cutlery that ought to work, so don't bother getting any silverware."

"Very well."

That settled, he turned to leave. The women would feed the workers, and he could make himself scarce by continuing to work on the interior of the house. He said over his shoulder, "I'll also have the boys plow a garden for you once they're done cleaning the stable."

"Thank you!"

"I'll have the buckboard here in ten minutes."

"Make it twenty minutes, Mr. Diamond. I have cinnamon rolls in the oven."

&a

Lorelei laughed at how the pots rattled and the toy wagon wheel squeaked as she pulled it up the road. The combination made for a comical symphony, and she delighted in the music because it reminded her of how God provided this opportunity for them to make money. This wasn't a tiny sum, either—it was enough to provide for a little while.

Mama would be coming in ten minutes, after the tarts came out of the oven. The men could start in on the main part of the meal first.

Mr. Diamond left his buckboard parked in the yard to serve

as a buffet table of sorts. She reached it, spread a cheery scarlet tablecloth over the bed, and started arranging the dishes.

"Chow time!" one of the men hollered to the others.

It wasn't necessary for him to shout. Two of the men had seen her coming and whistled. Part of her wanted to smile at how silly it was for them to do that, but the other part felt embarrassed. It didn't feel any better to have them all crowding around as she put a big roasting pan on the buckboard table.

"What did you fix us?"

"Today," she said as she picked up a kettle and a big saucepan by their handles and plunked them on either side of the roaster, "is pot roast, braised potatoes and baked carrots, peas, salad, and rolls."

"Got any gravy?"

"In the speckled pot that's still in my wagon." She didn't bother to get it. No less than three men dove to grab the gravy. They were all hardworking men, but when it came to food, they acted like starving little boys.

Old Mr. Bayley cast a woebegone look at the now-empty wagon. "No dessert?"

Lorelei smiled. He was such a nice man. "Mama knows you like berry tarts. She's taking them out of the oven in a few minutes."

The men heaped food on their plates and sat in the dirt to eat. Mr. Diamond wasn't anywhere to be seen, and Lorelei feared the men would dive in for seconds before he had a chance to get anything. She took a plate, placed generous portions of everything on it, and went around the back of the house toward what she'd learned was the kitchen.

A chair propped the back door open. "Mr. Diamond! I'm leaving food here for you." She stayed on the doorstep and peeked inside. The kitchen was homey, and the scarred cutting board made Lorelei think many happy hours had been spent in this room. The sensibly arranged room held a huge, ancient stove. Beside it lay a bedraggled-looking, heavily bandaged dog.

"Oh, you poor baby!" She remained outside, set the plate on the chair, and tugged a little piece of the roast free. "Here, puppy. Are you hungry?"

The dog barely paused to sniff, then gobbled it. The very tip of her tail, free of a bandage, swished to and fro in a sign of pleasure.

"What are you doing in here?"

Lorelei jumped at the harsh sound of Mr. Diamond's voice and whirled to face him. "You were not there. I saved food for you."

"You don't belong here."

He cast a disparaging look at the food and made an impatient sound. "Not just here in the house. You don't belong up here at all. You had to hear the men whistling at you."

Embarrassment washed from her bosom to her scalp in a scorching wave.

"It's foolhardy for you to deliver dinner alone. I hired your mother, not you. From now on, she's to bring the food. You can come only if she's with you."

"You are here, as is Mr. Bayley. I am safe enough."

"No one is ever safe." His voice rang with pain and bitterness.

"God is with me."

His face hardened, and his eyes narrowed as he shot back, "Where was God when your father died?"

❧

Russell helped Mrs. Goetz put the empty dishes from yet another fine meal into the wagon. Today's corned beef and cabbage, soda bread, and carrot cake tasted wonderful. Truth be told, she'd managed to bring something different every day so far, each meal far surpassing what he'd expected when they struck their bargain.

Rationing and food "rules" restricted what women cooked. Mrs. Goetz studiously adhered to the government's recommendations, but it never seemed as if her meals lacked anything at all. Fish and fowl dominated the menu instead of beef—just as the pamphlets advised. On "Meatless Mondays," she made hearty soup from Lorelei's vegetable garden or filling casseroles. On "Wheatless Wednesdays," she'd serve chicken with potatoes or rice and make puddings or baked apples for dessert. With sugar and butter being limited so more could be sent overseas, she still managed to use honey, molasses, currants and raisins, and cooking oil so creatively, the men actually asked for the recipes for their wives to use.

She deserved praise for her hard work, but Russell wasn't in much of a mood to talk.

"I'm leaving this here for your dog." Mrs. Goetz set a small earthenware bowl on the buckboard. "Lorelei scraped from yesterday's chicken bones the marrow and made a special gruel. It helps the puppy grow healthy again."

"Thanks."

"Lori and I—we are grateful to you for plowing the garden for us."

"She was planting stuff yesterday."

"No. She was mixing in ash and horse droppings to enrich the soil." Mrs. Goetz curled her fingers through the handle of the toy wagon and crammed her other fist into her apron pocket. "She will have to come with me here tomorrow for to get the buckboard. I must go to town for more food, and I do not drive."

It was the first time anything had been said about Lorelei not coming up to the house anymore. For a whole week, she'd stayed down at the cottage. Clearly, Lorelei helped cook the enormous meals, but never once had she ventured anywhere near the mansion.

Russell fought with himself over whether to go talk to her. He'd spoken in anger, and in doing so, he'd caused her grief to deepen. The memories of how she'd flinched at his words and the tears that filled her eyes haunted him. Her hand had trembled as she lifted it to touch the small silver cross hanging on a fragile chain about her neck. *Almost as if she were trying to shield her faith from my cruel onslaught.*

"How many more days do you need me to make the lunches? It looks good—this roof of yours. The men are working hard and fast. They will be done soon."

"Another week." He cleared his throat. "They'll also be repairing your roof and chimney, but I'll do the porch, myself."

Mrs. Goetz shook her head. "No."

"I understand you're worried about whether it's safe to have the men there. Perhaps you could make a few meals ahead and go into town with your daughter so she's not around them."

"This is not the problem." Aching pride showed in her careworn face and squared shoulders. "We do not want anything from you."

"What's that supposed to mean? It's my property. I'll do whatever I deem fit."

Tears silvered her eyes, making him remember how Lorelei's had glistened. "Patching a porch does not fix hurt feelings."

He inwardly winced at that observation and didn't pretend to misunderstand what she was saying. "I made your daughter cry. It won't happen again."

"My Lori has a big heart. She cares easily for others."

He shook his head. "Not after how I spoke to her. She's been glad to keep her distance."

"That is where you are wrong, Russell. Lorelei wants to bear your burden as a Christian should, but you have made it clear you want nothing to do with her or with God."

"She's not responsible for me or my soul."

"You are responsible for your soul," the older woman said in a matter-of-fact tone. "But as Christ's followers, we believe we are our brother's keepers. You were trying to be mindful of her safety when you told her not to come alone." She hitched her shoulder. "That time, you were being your sister's keeper."

Her comment didn't amuse him. "I upset her. You can tell her I'm sorry. Warn her I'm going to work on the porch so she can avoid me."

"Lorelei needs no warning. Perfect love—the kind God gives us in His name that we are to show one another—this special caring knows no fear."

Mrs. Goetz left, pulling the wagon behind her. Russell watched her leave. What would it be like to live without fear?

❧

"Here, girl. Come to me. Yes. Good girl." Lorelei crooned softly to the dog and knelt to capture her. No longer bandaged, the brown-and-white mutt still looked. . .well, like a mutt. One ear cocked up while the other flopped to the side. One haunch bore partially healed scrapes and was missing most of the fur. "What are you doing out alone?"

Lorelei gathered her in the basket of her arms, rose, and realized she'd never be able to carry the dog back to Mr. Diamond's house. He cared for this dog, and once he discovered she was missing, he'd be worried. Lorelei's gaze fell on the wagon. She managed to lay the dog in it, then worried it might hop out once the wheel started squeaking. Once she finished tying down the dog, she grabbed the handle, steeled herself with a deep breath, and headed toward the forbidden mansion.

Soon, she started to sing:

Are you ever burdened with a load of care?
Does the cross seem heavy you are called to bear?

Count your many blessings, every doubt will fly,
And you will be singing as the days go by.

"What are you. . ." Mr. Diamond's voice died out as he strode down the drive. His gait seemed steadier, his limp far less noticeable. His forehead creased, then he let out a disbelieving bark of a laugh. "My dog is wearing your apron?"

nine

"It was the only way I could be sure she wouldn't bound out. She is healing well, but I didn't think her strong enough to walk back here." Lorelei started to untie the apron strings she'd wound around the wagon to keep the dog inside.

Mr. Diamond knelt on the other side of the wagon and loosened a stubborn knot. "How did you get out, girl?"

The dog woofed and licked his hand.

"She probably smelled your cooking. I can't blame her for following her nose. Old Pinkus Bayley told me the men are taking their time to do a good job, but they might be working a tad slower than usual because of the food you're making."

"Mr. Bayley is a kindhearted man."

"And I'm not."

His words jolted Lorelei. She didn't know what to say. *Jesus, please give me the right words. I need Your wisdom and kindness.*

Mr. Diamond looked at her and said gruffly, "I'm not proud of how things went last week. I had no call to say what I did. Whatever gentility I once had is long gone. Stay away from me. I had the good sense to leave home so I wouldn't hurt those I love; this is my refuge. Once I have this place fixed, I won't have to bother with anyone else."

"It is no sin to hurt inside or to question God, Mr. Diamond." Her apron wadded in her hands as she quietly confessed, "God has heard more than a few of my questions and knows my grief. I would be wrong to judge you, let alone find you guilty of what I have done, myself."

"I saw your tears." Each word grated out of him. "You walked out of my kitchen weeping—because of me."

She closed her eyes for a moment, then opened them. "It was because of you. In this, you are right; but you are also wrong. I didn't cry for myself. I cried because I cannot imagine the pain you try to bear alone. In Psalms, it says the Good Shepherd is with us when we walk through the valley of the shadow of death. Many days and nights—even in the midst of my sorrow and questions—that has been my only comfort. I have been angry, and I have asked 'why?' but I have always leaned on the assurance that God is beside me. My heart aches to think you are without that comfort."

"You can't expect me to find peace when I've lived though war."

"Peace is not a place; it is a serenity that comes when we trust God that He will make all things right in His time."

He shook his head sadly. "Buttercup, I meant it. Keep your distance."

Buttercup—I like that he called me such a beautiful name. Deep inside, this man longs for good things. She reached out to pet his dog. "When you doctored her and bandaged her, did she try to bite you?"

Lightning fast, he reacted. "I'm not a stray dog for you to heal."

"No, you are not, but just as you understood she didn't mean to hurt you, I also accept that you reacted out of pain. Now that I see what is in your heart, I'm not afraid."

Pinkus sauntered up. "Good, good. The two of you are talking. Lorelei, knock some sense into this stubborn man's head. Tell him to hire me to paint the place after you put in the new windows."

Lorelei felt her face grow warm. "I cannot do this, Mr. Bayley." She'd secretly hoped Mr. Diamond would give her the commission to replace his broken windows. The job would bring in enough money for her to slip some into the savings sock. Now, though, since Mr. Diamond had made it clear he wanted nothing to do with her, she couldn't very well make a bid for the work.

"Why not?" The old man's face crinkled into a hundred wrinkles as he turned to Russell. "You unhappy with the job my men have been doing?"

"I'm pleased. The roof and chimneys look good."

"Then what's the holdup? While we do the roof and chimney over at the cottage, Lorelei can get to work on your windows up here."

"I didn't order the paint yet," Mr. Diamond said.

Something about the set of his jaw made Lorelei take a second look. He put down the dog, and as the dog gingerly tested standing again, realization dawned. *He's offended because his leg is weak. Climbing the ladder will be too hard, but he doesn't want anyone to treat him like a cripple.*

Lorelei sat in the wagon and folded her hands in her lap. "What colors did you decide on, Mr. Diamond? When you paint the inside of your house, will you do different colors for the rooms?"

"He can paint them whatever color he fancies. Don't make no nevermind to me," Mr. Bayley snorted. "And the outside—well, to my way of thinking, it would be a crying shame to paint this grand old woman anything other than white." He directed his attention back toward Mr. Diamond. "Russ, reason it through. By the time you buy ladders and scaffolding, you pert near hired my crew to do the outside of this place. They could really use the work, and you have plenty that needs doing on the inside to keep you busy."

Clearly, the old man's reasoning went a long way toward salvaging Mr. Diamond's pride. Mr. Diamond hooked his thumbs through belt loops and drawled, "Slate. I want slate for some of the detail work."

"Slate blue, or slate gray?" Lorelei ruffled the fur between the dog's ears.

"Isn't it the same?" both men asked in unison.

She shook her head. "What colors do you want inside?"

"Back to that, eh?" Bayley chuckled.

"Well, if he wants to use silver, pink, and black inside, then he should use slate gray." She tilted her head toward Mr. Diamond. "If you want to use blues, lavender, and gold, you should use blue slate."

"Sounds to me like the lass knows what she's talking about. She going to do the windows before we set to painting?"

"I need to go back home." Lorelei wondered why she'd bothered to try to look so casual. She stood and reached for the wagon handle, the whole time feeling embarrassed that her neighbor didn't want her around and hadn't offered her the job. "Good-bye."

"What's awrong with her?" Mr. Bayley muttered as she dragged the wagon down the gravel.

Mr. Diamond mumbled something, but Lorelei couldn't tell precisely what he said. Then again, maybe that was best. *Perhaps he has been too polite to say it, but the real reason he doesn't want me around is the same reason others have shunned us. Yes, he asked Mama to cook, but he was desperate. The truth is, he doesn't think I'm American; he thinks I am the enemy.*

❧

"Miss Goetz?" Russell stood in the doorway of what looked to be her workshop. Lorelei was welding something on a table, and he'd waited until she put the soldering iron down so she wouldn't burn herself. In those moments, he promised himself that he'd mind his words so he didn't hurt her again.

"Yes?" She glanced over her shoulder at him.

"I'd like to speak with you."

"Come around toward the window." She swept her hand in a fluid gesture. "I have not swept and do not want you to get glass in your shoes."

He walked around the perimeter of the room and hated how his uneven gait sounded on the cement floor. If Lorelei noticed it, she managed to hide her reaction. She sat on a tall stool, had a pencil shoved haphazardly into her hair, and wore a supple leather apron that nearly covered her everyday dress.

As far as he knew, she owned three dresses—a "Sunday-best" gray-and-black one and two "everyday" dresses. He strongly suspected the sunshine-yellow dress had been her Sunday-best until she'd needed to make the gray-and-black-striped one for mourning.

"What are you making?"

She fussed with the edge of the window. "A piece for the Mariners' Chapel."

"Can we hold it up so I can see the design?"

"I need to weld a few more places before it can be moved."

"Okay. I'll wait." He watched as she exchanged the soldering iron for another that she had waiting on a potbelly-type affair. Even with all the windows and both doors open, the heat made the workroom feel sticky and hot. *But that thing isn't enough to keep this big, drafty room warm in the winter. I'll have to put in a larger one. Maybe she'd rather have a second one in the opposite corner.*

"There's another stool. You are welcome to have a seat." She bent over her task and concentrated on each action with precision that made her features take on an intensity that caused her eyes to glow. The heat from soldering and her passion for what she did made her cheeks rosy.

"You love what you do."

"It was a gift from my papa. He taught me."

He didn't want to talk about her father. He'd seen too

much death in his short time in the trenches to want to think of it now. Instead, Russell tried to keep the conversation focused on her work. "What is this one called?"

"Fishers of Men."

"Do you design them yourself, or do you have a book of samples?"

"Each window is a new opportunity. I talk to the person who commissions it and see what they have in mind, then I make sketches and have them select what pleases them." She handled the flux, soldering wire, and iron with a deftness that bespoke many hours of practice.

"The racks there for storing your glass are clever."

She laughed. "You are teasing me."

"I'm serious." He looked at the wooden fixtures that held a veritable rainbow of glass panes in and orderly vertical array. *The attorney said my uncle feared her place might be vandalized. No wonder he worried. All this glass. . .*

"Every business has to organize the material," she said in a practical tone.

Her words pulled him away from imagining what danger she and her mother might have been in, in town. He didn't want to think of that, and conversing about how she had things set up seemed easy enough. "You can see everything, and it doesn't take much storage space."

She glanced up from her work. Her eyes danced with unrestrained humor. "Some were broken when we moved here, so I use noodle drying racks on the end to hold the smaller pieces."

"Noodle drying racks?" He took a closer look. "No wonder you thought I was teasing you."

Setting aside the soldering iron, she offered, "We can lift this now so you can see it if you are still interested."

"Let me help."

"Just a minute, please." She rotated a crank, and a length

of sturdy rope snaked down from a pulley hanging from a ceiling beam. The rope forked into two equal lengths. Each held substantial hooks. "This will make it easy." She stood on one of the rungs of her stool and stretched forward as far as she could.

"I'm closer." He took the hooks and threaded them through rings she'd affixed to the top of the window. "There."

Slowly, carefully, she operated the crank until the window hung suspended in space. "Come to this side so you can see the sun coming through the panes."

Russell didn't need to be asked twice. He'd already gotten the general flavor of the piece and wanted to see its full splendor. He reached her side and looked at the work in awe. Boats floated on rippled glass that looked just like water. The fishes' scales were iridescent, and the faces on Christ and the men He'd called to become his disciples had been painted with undeniable artistry. "Incredible."

"You like it?" She watched him eagerly, clearly wanting to see his reaction.

"That belongs in a museum."

"There is a second one." The implicit offer came out in a shy admission.

"Show me!"

She left his side, went to another crank, and raised another piece off a nearby sturdy table. In the foreground, a young sailor gripped a ship's wheel. Jesus stood behind him, one hand on the sailor's shoulder, the other extended, pointing the way. The thin black paint stroked on the glass gave grain to the "wood," folds to the "cloth," and strands to "hair."

"You're such a wonderful artist. What will you do for my house?"

Lorelei gave him a wary look.

"You don't just do religious windows, do you? What about

something old-fashioned?"

"You would have to show me which window." She still looked less than eager.

"Lorelei—I'd like to call you by your given name, if you don't mind." She nodded her permission. "I couldn't put you in a dangerous situation. I worried you might get hurt, climbing a ladder and trying to glaze the windows."

"That is not the only reason." She turned away. Her shoulders were hiked clear up to her ears with the tension that sang through her. "I would not have a lie between us. It is better to be honest, even when it hurts."

He sighed. "All right. I'm sure you guessed it anyway. Your mom and I had a discussion. You've got a tender heart, Lorelei. I decided to keep my distance because I don't want my bitterness to poison you."

"Then why are you here now?"

"Because Pinkus showed me how I can remove the window frames and bring them to you. You'll be working from home, and I won't show up if I'm in a bad mood."

She looked doubtful, so he pressed, "Next week, while the men are working on your roof and chimney, you and your mom can come to my place. You can number all of the windows and measure them. We can decide on some of the places to hang some of these masterpieces, then we'll all go to town and buy whatever glass and supplies you'll need."

"Tell me, Mr. Diamond—"

"Russell. Call me Russell."

"Tell me, Russell." She paused as if to bolster her nerve, then blurted out, "Do you really want us at your home? Many do not, because they think we are German."

❧

"I'm English and Irish; you're German. We're both American." His answer came too quickly—as if he'd rehearsed it.

Lorelei paused. *Do I want to pursue this or let it go?*

He shifted his weight and looked uncomfortable. Her silence must have prodded him because he began to speak again. "I admit, the first time you spoke and I heard your accent, it surprised me."

"It was not a happy surprise."

He exhaled slowly. "No, it wasn't. I won't bother lying. Heines. Huns. Krauts—I've heard it all, and I've even said it, myself. Living like a rat in trenches, soldiers are crude and desperate. They have to build up hatred so they can kill the enemy. It isn't easy to come home and hear echoes of your enemy in your neighbor's voice."

ten

"I am not your enemy."

"Of course you aren't. I've come to know that full well." Russell's features tautened. "I've seen the gold star in your window. I know you've paid the ultimate price for our country."

Lorelei bowed her head. Her eyes and nose stung with tears. "Papa wanted to go. He loved America and wanted to help."

Russell cleared his throat. "Then there's no problem with me hiring you to replace my windows or commission stained glass—unless you're already backlogged."

"'Fishers of Men' was the last piece I had on order." She pasted a brave smile on her face and hoped he wouldn't ask why she didn't have stacks of orders waiting. Before the war, they were always backlogged with commissions; now, no one wanted to do business with German Americans.

Russell nodded. "It's selfish, but I'm glad. I need you to work for me."

"I am able to start on your house right away."

"I have to go get paint in a few days. We can pick up some windowpanes while we're at it. How do you keep the glass from breaking when you transport it?"

"It's not easy. Sometimes, one of the neighbors who has a motorcar drives for me. When we moved here, I layered straw in the bed of a wagon, then laid the glass between our blankets." She cast a glance at the noodle drying racks. "The pieces that broke, I kept. I can use them still."

"Are you able to match glass?"

"Sometimes. Why do you ask?"

80

"There's a leaded-glass window in the parlor that has a few bars of color here and there. I like the effect, but about half of the window is broken. Temporarily, I'll have you replace the whole thing with plain glass, but eventually, I'd like to have you restore it."

"If you show me, I can see what kind of glass it is. Even if there is none in town, we could put in a special order. I should warn you, red glass is most expensive. Gold is used to make the red glass, thought it would not seem so to look at it."

He gave her a look she couldn't interpret, and Lorelei felt gauche for having to broach the subject. "You have much work to do, and the cost must be a great burden. I wanted to let you know so I can keep my windows for you affordable."

"I see."

"I could replace the regular windows for you first, because those will be cheapest. When the new garden plot begins to yield a harvest, Mama and I can sell your share or can it for you, and you will end up with a little bit more money."

He scanned her workshop and pointed at a dowel. "What are those metal, snake-like things?"

"Lead cames. They are the channels the glass fits into and come in different widths and shapes. The U shape is for the edges, and the H shape is for the middle." She smiled. "Like when you put together a puzzle—the inside pieces must have nooks and crannies to hold onto one another, but the border must be smooth."

"When I got here, you were using solder and flux."

"Yes." *Such an intelligent man, gathering information so he can calculate the costs of materials.* "When I do more delicate work, I sometimes use copper foil. If you have any lamps which are in need of repair, that would probably be the technique I would employ."

"Where do you buy all of this stuff?"

"The store is starting to order it for me again." As soon as the words were out of her mouth, Lorelei regretted them.

Russell's eyes narrowed. "Starting to? What does that mean?"

"It is of no consequence now."

He tilted her face up to his. "They persecuted you for being German, didn't they?"

"No longer. And during the time I needed things, Mr. Bayley was most helpful. He very kindly used his connections with stores in other towns to obtain whatever I lacked."

"So the old codger is really a guardian angel in disguise, huh?"

Russell's tone was warm and rich with approval, so the words didn't seem disrespectful in the least. Lorelei smiled and nodded.

"We'll go to town day after tomorrow." She detected a slight edge to his voice as he added, "Make a list. Don't worry about which stores we'll go to."

"I need to ask Mama. She might need my help with the cooking or something."

"Lorelei, it would have been dishonorable for me to come speak with you if I hadn't already gotten her approval."

"Oh." She looked into his unfathomable eyes. "I did not mean to insult your integrity."

"No offense taken."

"Well?" Mama stood in the doorway. "What do you—oh, Lori! The window *ist wunderbar!*"

"You like it?" Lorelei vacillated between being delighted that her mother loved the work and being worried that Russell would get upset at hearing a few German words.

"*Ja!*" Mama waggled her finger at Russell. "I told you my girl, she makes beautiful windows."

"She does. I'll be here day after tomorrow to take her to get supplies. Perhaps you could come with us to the house now so she can get a feel for what she's going to need."

"I cannot go. I have food almost ready for the stove—potato soup, green beans fresh from the garden, and bread, of course. It is just humble food, but perhaps you should eat supper here."

Lorelei watched indecision flit across his handsome features. "Put it in the wagon. You can use my stove. I need to fire up the oven, anyway. Mutt is sleeping next to it at night."

"This is good, yes. We can come together this way." Mama bobbed her head approvingly. She spun about and headed back to their cottage.

Russell sat on a stool, out of the way as Lorelei took care of the small oven so the fire would go out, then let down the stained-glass windows and put things away. "Where's your broom, Lorelei?"

She shook her head. "I am odd. I prefer to sweep in the morning, before I start to work. The little slivers of glass welcome me, and I like the way the morning sun turns them all into sparkles. It makes me happy to start to work again each day."

"Are we ready?" Mama stood in the doorway again.

"Not yet." Russell slid off the stool. "I'm virtually living in the dark. I have one lamp. It would probably be wise for us to take one of your lamps or a candle along so I can get you back here safely."

Lorelei slanted him a funny look. "This, coming from a man who leaves logs in our woodpile at night?"

❧

Russell woke, rolled out of bed, and grimaced as his leg cramped. He'd overdone yesterday, and he'd pay for it dearly today; but since he'd spoken with Lorelei and they'd cleared the air, he felt better.

He'd wondered yesterday if she'd just been in a good mood after finishing that incredible window, so he'd gone down to the garden and tried to act casual as he watched her garden.

"Russell! Hello!" Lorelei's warm smile had drawn him closer.

"I'll hold that." He took the bucket off her arm and watched as she deftly started filling it with beans. To his surprise, the smell of soil didn't bother him. He'd absently picked some of the string beans and added them to the harvest. After that, they each filled a whole basket with tomatoes. He'd spoken very little; she chattered sunnily and hummed under her breath. Contentment radiated from her, and he'd basked in it.

Unwilling to lose the ease he found in her company, he'd urged her to come measure more windows last evening before they'd make the trip to buy supplies. Mrs. Goetz invited herself along and again made supper for all of them, then puttered around the downstairs as if she belonged there. Only after she left did he discover Mrs. Goetz had worked wonders in the parlor.

Rubbing the morning stubble on his face and staring down at the fresh scars on his leg, he willed away the pain—but the pain didn't obey. The doctors removed whatever shrapnel they could, and they'd set his leg—but his leg had healed an inch shorter, and some of the shrapnel remained in place.

I have my leg. I'll take the pain. Russell shuddered at the memory of them discussing amputation. He'd shouted himself raw, telling them not to do it. In the end, they'd been worried about infection and damaging nerves, so they'd left shrapnel behind—a permanent reminder of war. . .*as if my memories and limp aren't enough.*

In a sour mood, he glared at daybreak's first ribbons of light streaming through the window. The blanket that normally hung there was missing, and he jolted. The windows! Today, he and Lorelei would go into the village and get the supplies to do more work on his house.

Dressed, but with his shirt hanging open, Russell hobbled into his kitchen. The aroma of coffee sped his uneven gait. Mutt's head lifted, and her ears perked up. Slowly, she struggled to her feet and headed for the door. Russell let her out and grinned at the stove.

Just before she left last night, Lorelei had put a pot of coffee on the back of the stove. "It has far too much water. During the night, the banked embers in the stove will cause the extra water to steam away. You will start your day with a good cup of coffee."

Mmm. He reached for a cup and could hardly wait to get a mouthful. It was a fine trick—one he'd remember, just as he'd keep a big kettle of water on the stove each night so he'd have warm water with which to wash and shave in the mornings.

By the time he hitched the horses and drove the buckboard to the cottage, Russell came to a stunning realization: For the first time since he'd come home, he didn't mind being with other people.

Well, not exactly. He didn't want to cope with everyone in town, but he found an odd comfort in Lorelei's company and an undemanding nurturing in her mother's presence. Odd, but he felt a kinship with them: they didn't want to have to interact with some of the people in town any more than he did. *If Lorelei can face those people, I can, too.*

❧

Lorelei laughed the minute Russell drove up. "So you brought your friend?"

He twisted and urged the dog to sit in the back of the buckboard. "Silly dog is starting to follow me everywhere. She jumped aboard as I was leaving."

"You have doctored her well, that she can jump." She hefted a bushel of vegetables and swung it into the buckboard. "Mama said you told her we could take the produce to town to sell."

Russell got down and wrested the next bushel from her. "Give me that."

Mama came out of the cottage, crossed the brand new, brick-edged, cement veranda he'd made, and started for the buckboard. Russell made an irritated sound, went to her, and grabbed the box of quart-sized canning jars from her. "What do you think you're doing?"

"Taking the produce to town, as you told me I could." She toddled along beside him. "You brought the dog. Do you think whoever the owner is will claim her?"

He stiffened for an instant, then shrugged. "We'll see."

Once they reached town, it didn't take long to unload the produce at the mercantile. The money went toward their store account, so Lorelei turned toward the paint. Russell stopped her. "Did you need anything?"

"Not today, thank you."

He stared at her, then asked in an undertone, "I should have asked before we got here. What do you need?"

"Just two days ago, Mama and I came with your buckboard to buy the food to feed your workers. Our kitchen is quite full. If you have the paint, we can go on to get the glass."

"Okay."

Russell barely finished loading the paint into the buckboard when an energetic group of boys raced up and encircled him. "Is it true? Were you in the war? Did you kill a bunch of Krauts?"

Lorelei saw sweat bead on his forehead and upper lip as the boys continued to pepper him with questions. The haunted look about his eyes intensified, yet he remained completely silent.

"We want to hear all about it!"

"Not from me." Russell pushed past them and helped Mama into the buckboard.

"Heroes do not boast, boys," Lorelei said softly as she slipped past the boys. As they drove off, she leaned forward and whispered to Russell, "We can get the glass another day."

"No." His voice was low and harsh. "Whatever needs doing is getting done on this trip."

eleven

Lorelei rolled the putty into a long, smooth, snake-like cord, then carefully positioned it along the edge of the glass. Once she it lay in place, she used her putty knife and pressed the doughy substance into place and smoothed it so the seal would be sound and the glass secure.

Windowpane after windowpane, she'd done this. A simple skill, glazing a window didn't take a lot of thought, but each one gave her a sense of satisfaction. This particular window sash held four panes; two were originals, and she'd replaced the other pair. The original ones had a faint undertone of lavender to them, and she'd searched among all of the panes of available glass to match it. Old glass often had ripples, bubbles, or tint to it, and on the day they'd gone to buy glass, Russell said he wanted to restore the house to be comfortably livable, but have it maintain its old flair. He'd been genuinely pleased at the notion of trying to approximate color matches instead of doing wholesale replacement of all of the windows.

Russell. Ever since that day when the boys wanted him to talk about the war, he's become more reserved.

"Ready for lunch?" Mama asked from behind her.

"In just a minute."

Mama's footsteps died out, and Lorelei carefully replaced the lid on the putty can before going to the cottage. Once there, she washed up.

"You stopped singing today," Mama said as she fished corn on the cob from the kettle with a pair of tongs. "Usually, you sing as you work. What worries you?"

"Russell."

"Ahhh." Mama's voice held a wealth of understanding.

"For awhile, I thought maybe he just needed to meet people. He started being more sociable for a little while, but then he got grumpy again. He's all by himself up at that house, day in and day out. It's not good, Mama."

"He's hurting. Not his leg—his heart. Men who go to fight can do this. Some call it 'shell shocked,' but he is not crazy in the head or dangerous. He has curled away from the world because his soul is wounded."

"His soul won't heal if he doesn't read his Bible or go to church, but I can't push him. I feel like God is asking me to be patient and gentle with him."

"God reveals Himself in many ways. It is for us to be right with the Lord so we can be light in the darkness."

"He won't talk at all about the war."

"I can imagine why not. A man who has witnessed the brutality of combat can bear wounds that only the Lord sees. Deep wounds don't heal rapidly."

"He came here to get away from those he loves. He told me he did it so he wouldn't hurt them. Perhaps this is a relapse of the pain that initially brought him to this place."

"We will pray. God is faithful. He will not let this warrior's wounds fester forever. There will come a time of healing."

"That is what is needed," Lorelei agreed. "A prayer for restoration."

❦

The smell of sawdust filled the air. Russell moved down one more step and started to sand the next balustrade. Mutt scooted down beside him. The dog shadowed his every move. Russell surveyed his work. He'd gotten almost all of this side of the stairs done; the other side had taken four days. Inch by inch, he'd been stripping varnish, sanding, pulling the wood in the house down to bare grain.

The wind off the ocean felt far stiffer today. He welcomed the refreshing change. Most of the month, record-breaking temperatures had scorched the coast. The marble floor of the entryway helped keep the center portion of the house cooler, so he'd purposefully planned to work in this area during the peak of the heat.

The sound of glasses clinking together made him pause.

"Russell!" Lorelei stood in the open front door with a huge smile on her face. "Look at how much work you have done!"

Mutt gave a happy yip of recognition and scuttled down the stairs to her side.

Russell stood and dusted off the front of his shirt and sleeves. "No, look at how much work *you've* done." He walked toward her and shook his head. "I told you, I don't need this."

"We agreed to sharecrop." She pressed the crate into his arms. "You will not take your portion of the money; the least we can do is see to it you have food put up in your pantry. Mama said you are to come to supper tonight."

"Your mother would have me eat supper with you every night. She must think I'm starving."

Lorelei laughed as she passed the crate full of jars to him. "Can you blame her? We saw the charcoal you tried to feed this dog. If that is your idea of a roast, it is a wonder both of you survive!"

The sound of horses made them both turn around. Pinkus Bayley rode right up to the veranda. "Folks," he greeted them curtly, "'member how I insisted on the men making new storm shutters? Well, I brought the liveryman's boys to help you get 'em up and batten down the hatches. We've got us a big storm brewin', and the drop on my barometer makes me think it'll be a hurricane."

"Oh, my." The color drained from Lorelei's face. "I have heard they are fearsome things."

"Never been in one?" Pinkus shook his head. "Lock the covers on your wells to keep debris out, and board up the windows. You got a basement, just in case it gets bad?"

Russell set aside the jars. "I do. Lorelei, run down to get your mother. Grab kerosene, lamps, candles, and some blankets. Haul it back here in the wagon." He shook the old man's hand. "Thanks for rounding up help."

"Glad to do it." Pinkus nodded. "Those of us on the windward side of town are seeing boats make for storm anchor, but I reckoned those of you out here didn't know. Ships are reporting North Carolina's getting hit hard, and they've measured higher than thirty-four knot winds. Hurricane flags went up an hour ago. I'm going on to warn the Rimmons."

Four hours later, the boys had fastened the storm shutters built onto the upper windows and affixed the ones made for the lower ones. Russell helped them board up the windows down at the Goetzes' cottage. The boys had refused his offer to stay, delightedly accepted five dollar bills a piece as payment, and ridden back home.

"I just filled the bathtub," Lorelei called from upstairs as he came inside. "It's cold in the basement. If you don't mind, I'll take the blankets from your beds and drop them down to you."

"There's only one bed. It's in the last room on the right." He turned as Mrs. Goetz emerged from the basement. "Is the fire in the stove out?"

"Ja. But first, I made a good stew and plenty of hot coffee. We will have a good meal as we endure this storm, but I have closed the flue so we will not have smoke come in."

The winds had been picking up steadily. Soon they shrieked, and rain pelted the house. As it sat atop a hill overlooking the ocean, the house groaned in the fury. He'd put if off for as long as he could, but Russell knew the time had come. He led the women to the basement door, sent them down along with the dog, then stared into the dank, dusty darkness. He broke out in a cold sweat. *It's like the trenches.*

twelve

Wind howled louder. Lorelei pulled her sweater closed more for comfort than for warmth as Russell shut the door and descended the steps. She saw his steps falter. *His leg! The steps are steep, and it's dark.*

Lorelei grabbed a lamp and hastened to the base of the stairs to light his way. She forced a laugh. "Promise you won't be mad when you get down here and see where Mutt is."

Russell paused and scanned the dim basement.

"Look at the cot."

"We need more light in here." His harsh words echoed in the enclosed space.

"*Ja,* this I am seeing to." Mama laughed. "Seeing to—that was funny." She turned with two more lighted lamps, came toward the stairs, and handed one to Russell.

He breathes too fast. His face is sweaty. Lorelei shuffled back a bit. "You've worked hard for our safety, and we're trapping you on those stairs. Come. Sit and rest now."

He descended the last step and made a sharp turn to the left. Wordlessly, he prowled the basement, inspecting every last inch. The stairs marked the center of a narrow, fifteen-foot room. One end opened into a small, square room.

"This room, since it already has shelves, we thought was perfect for storing everything." Lorelei scanned what had probably served as an additional pantry in years gone by. "Do you think we have enough?"

Russell barely paid attention to the crate of canned food, the odd assortment of buckets and pitchers filled with water, or the folded stack of blankets. He grabbed a tin of kerosene and shook it. "Almost full."

"Yes. We also brought a box of candles." *Why is he so concerned about light?*

He exited the storage room and looked about as if he hadn't seen the main room before. He walked the full length and stopped by the clunky vacuum cleaner.

"Mama, she coughs when she gets around too much dust," Lorelei said. "I didn't have time enough to clean well, but the worst of the dust is gathered and gone."

He nodded. "There's not much of anything down here."

Mama sat down in one of the three chairs they'd brought down and patted the seat of another. "Come. Sit. Lorelei is right. You have worked hard. There is nothing to do now but wait."

Russell shook his head. "Things down here look fine for a fall-back position if the need is present. For now, we'll stay in the entryway."

"But is that safe?" Mama fretted.

He'd already started toward the stairs. "It's in the center of the house, away from the wind pattern."

Lorelei and her mother exchanged baffled glances.

"Hand me the coffee pot and the stew," Russell called from the top of the stairs. "I don't want you to spill and scorch yourselves."

They settled in the curved area of the entryway in the shelter of the staircase. Instead of sitting with them, Russell kept prowling around. He'd come back with something each time—an overstuffed chair from the parlor for Mama, a small table from the library for their food. After his fifth or sixth trip, Mama grabbed his arm.

"Come. Have coffee with us."

"Yes," Lorelei agreed. "You've done more than enough to make us safe and comfortable."

Russell sat on a wooden chair he'd brought from upstairs. He accepted a mug of coffee, curled his big, capable hands around it, and took a big gulp. Mutt settled on the floor beside him. "Raining pretty good out there now."

"Does that mean it's started?" Lorelei listened as the wind whistled through the shutters.

"Perhaps." He shrugged. "Hurricanes can also have bands of rain clouds that come before the brunt of the storm. We'll sit tight."

"This is a good place to be." Mama craned her neck and studied the area. "It is like being in the cleft of the rock. I don't remember where that is in the Bible."

"Exodus thirty-three." Russell jerked his cup up to his mouth and took another drink.

"Let's read it." Lorelei strove to hide her surprise at how quickly he'd rapped out the citation. She took a small Bible from the pocket of her apron. "I tucked this in before we left the house. Exodus thirty-three. . ." She ran her finger down the page until she reached the passage.

"Starting at verse twenty-one. 'And the LORD said, Behold, there is a place by me, and thou shalt stand upon a rock: And it shall come to pass, while my glory passeth by, that I will put thee in a cleft of the rock, and will cover thee with my hand while I pass by: And I will take away mine hand, and thou shalt see my back parts: but my face shall not be seen.'"

Russell didn't seem to be in the least bit interested in the Scripture, but the fact that he'd known precisely where to find the verse hinted that he'd spent considerable time in the Word at some point.

Mama began to hum. She paused and smiled at Russell. "This is your house. You do not mind if we sing, do you?"

He shrugged.

Mama began to sing, and Lorelei joined in:

A wonderful Savior is Jesus my Lord,
   A wonderful Savior to me;
He hideth my soul in the cleft of the rock,
   Where rivers of pleasure I see.

He hideth my soul in the cleft of the rock
   That shadows a dry, thirsty land;
He hideth my life with the depths of His love,
   And covers me there with His hand,
   And covers me there with His hand.

As they finished the last line, Russell leaned forward and reached for the coffeepot. Lorelei grabbed it and poured more for him. He'd tolerated the hymn, but clearly, he didn't enjoy the lyrics.

Instead of letting things fall into awkward silence, she said, "You've done much to the house. What will you do next?"

"I'm stripping the wood." He reached up and curled his fingers around one of the balustrades. "Think I'll strip wallpaper out of the parlor, then do a lot of staining and painting."

"The wallpaper is ready to come down in there," Mama agreed. "If you mix vinegar and water, then put it on the paper with a sponge, it will make the glue let go."

"Vinegar?"

Mama nodded. "The day you do this, you will smell like the pickles or sauerkraut."

When he chuckled, relief poured through Lorelei. She settled back. "What color will you paint the parlor, and what will you do about curtains?"

Gusts of wind and rain pelted the house. They discussed his plans, gave suggestions, and finally ate stew. When Mama yawned, Russell took a second lamp, lit it, and ordered Mutt to stay before he walked off.

"I think he's getting the cot, Mama. I'll go get the blankets from that little room in the basement."

"Do you need the lamp?"

"No, Russell has one. It'll only take a minute."

Lorelei descended the stairs, took a few steps, and let out a gasp as something knocked her to the floor and hands closed around her throat.

thirteen

"Rus-selllll." His name came out in a breathless whisper. It took another second for him to realize his assailant wasn't fighting back. Long strands of hair filled his hands, too. *Lorelei!*

Russell let go and rolled to his knees. "Are you all right?"

Lorelei lay there, her eyes huge with fright, yet she nodded.

"Can you breathe?" He anxiously brushed her hair back as remorse clawed at him.

"Yes."

"Did I hurt you? Can you move?"

She rolled to the side and started to push herself into a sitting position. "You surprised me is all."

Gently as he could, Russell pushed her back down. He dragged the kerosene lantern he'd left on the floor closer. Even as he gently turned her head so he could examine her neck, she protested.

"Truly, Russell, I am fine."

Fear turned to anger. "Why did you sneak up on me?"

"The blankets—they're down here."

"If I'd had another second or my trench knife, you'd be dead."

She shook her head and rested her hand on his arm. "No, Russell. You would never hurt me."

"Buttercup, you have more faith than brains." He stood and loomed over her. "Go back upstairs."

She took his hand and got to her feet. He braced her, afraid she might suddenly collapse, sick at the thought she'd cower from him. Lorelei rested her hand in the center of his chest—more, it seemed to still the thundering beneath her palm than

to steady herself. Standing there, she looked so fragile, so feminine. He'd scared the wits out of her, yet she smiled up at him
and acted as if her heartbeat didn't match his. Being down
here scared him; being around her scared him even more.

"I'll get the blankets, and you can get the cot," she decided.

He clamped his hands around her waist, lifted, and set her
halfway up the stairs. "Get going."

She took hold of the stair rail, so he let go and turned his
back on her.

"I'll wait here. If you go get the blankets, you can hand
them to me."

"Stubborn woman."

Her laughter warmed the basement. "Yes, I am."

She's not leaving me down here alone. Russell didn't know
whether to be relieved or mad. He strode to the small room,
grabbed the blankets, and stomped back. "Here. Scat."

"Yessir!" Humor tinted her voice.

He grabbed the cot he'd been folding, snatched the lamp,
and sped up the stairs. Though desperate to be out of there,
he still wasn't ready to let matters alone. Russell set up the
cot with a few practiced moves, then tugged Lorelei's hand.
She lost balance and tumbled into his arms with a surprised
cry. He lay her onto the cot.

"What is this?" Mrs. Goetz hopped to her feet.

"Loosen your daughter's collar and check her out. I practically
broke her neck." Russell paced away and kept his back turned.

*As soon as the storm's gone, they'll be gone—and I'll make sure
they don't come back. I could have killed her.*

❧

"A week," Lorelei grumbled under her breath. "A whole week,
and he still barely speaks to me." She scored the glass, tapped
along the underside with her cutting tool, then snapped it neatly
into two pieces. Ever since he set upon her in the basement,

Russell had kept his distance.

"Now, Lori," her mother chided as she cleaned one of the windows, "don't be so impatient. Russell Diamond is a good man. He's been very busy, clearing away all of those branches which fell—and didn't he cut them into logs for our very own fireplace and stove?"

"Yes, Mama. You don't have to convince me that he has many fine qualities."

"Well, you have been very busy, too. You were in town most every day, fixing windows that storm broke." Mama smiled. "I still thank God that it did not worsen and become all we feared."

"If that was a storm, I don't want to live through a hurricane!" Lorelei walked to the glass rack and selected a small scrap of green to use for a leaf. As she decided how to cut it to use the swirl pattern in the glass to its best advantage, she added, "God heard us when we were singing that He covered us with His hand."

Ja, so this is true." Mama finished the window and set aside her rag. "And what about the gardens? I thought for sure the plants would all blow away."

"Having the gardens by the hedges helped. They served as a windbreak. If you take produce in to town tomorrow, could you please tell Mr. Rawlin that this window is done? Maybe he can drive out to get it."

A shadow fell on the workroom. She glanced up. "Russell!"

"How big is the window?"

"Come see." She gestured to him.

He ordered Mutt to stay in the doorway, walked around the edge of the workroom as he had before, then came to her side to look at it. "Pretty, but not big at all."

"No, it's not." She nudged a piece into alignment. "Teddy broke one just like it when he was playing ball. It belongs to Miss Florina."

Russell winced. "I broke a neighbor's window once. Worked long and hard to pay for it." He stuffed his hands in his pockets and looked decidedly uncomfortable. "I. . .um. . .came to ask a favor."

"That is what neighbors are for."

"I don't know about that. I got a letter from home."

"Is everything okay?" Mama blurted out.

"Yes." He shot her a kind smile, and Lorelei liked him all the more for how nice he always was to Mama. "To put it in a nutshell, my mom and sister have decided they need to come see the house. It's nowhere near ready to have visitors, and I'm not even sure what I need to get."

"Curtains, towels, beds, and bedding for two rooms," Lorelei said at once.

"I like to sew." Mama smiled. "You get many yards of nice fabric, and I can make curtains and pillows and a cushion for a chair in each room."

Russell held his hand up in surrender. "Wait! I figured I'd have you come shopping with me tomorrow. We'll deliver the window while we're at it."

"Stay for supper. You need to eat better." Mama shook her finger at him and headed toward the door. "And come for breakfast. It will be a long day tomorrow."

❧

His head pounded unmercifully, his leg ached, and Russell knew they'd barely begun. He shot Lorelei a get-me-out-of-here glare.

"No, thank you, Mrs. Whorter. I am positive he won't want Chinese urns." She picked up a crystal vase and turned it toward the sun. It cast myriad rainbows about them. Unlike everything else in the store, it was American-made instead of imported. "This Heisey vase is the last thing. You will pack it with the rest so we can pick it up in an hour?"

"Yes. Of course." Mrs. Whorter set the vase on the counter

next to an appreciable pile of towels and toiletries, then gave her a shrewd look.

"Good. We've got to get moving." Russell got out of Whorter's Imports and collapsed on a bench on the boardwalk.

"This is moving?" Lorelei plopped down beside him and giggled.

"I have to recover. I kept wanting to sneeze." He scrubbed his hand across his nose to try to stop the tingling from all of the perfumed soaps, powders, and whatnots. "What's wrong with getting all of that stuff at the mercantile?"

"Nothing." Lorelei tugged on the edge of her glove. "But Mrs. Whorter is a widow, and it is nice to give her business. We can go to the mercantile after we go to the china shop—unless you want to use those everyday plates we already bought for when we were feeding the workmen."

"I'm only doing this once. Since I have your help, we'll get the fancy china today."

Ten minutes later, Lorelei somehow managed to get Mrs. Sweeny to seat Russell in a dining chair at a table. "Now, then," Lorelei said, "it is easier to picture the place setting."

She coordinated things that made it all go together so well—the Garland pattern of the Fostoria crystal carried the same graceful motion as the swags between the historical cameos on the Virginia pattern of the Lenox china. The Mount Vernon pattern of Lunt silverware featured the same style of curve.

Even a year ago, this would have irritated him to no end. Now, having a young lady set pretty things on the table before him, worry about whether it harmonized with the other pieces, the soft rise and fall of her sweet voice, the graceful little gestures—it all rolled over him like a balm. War did that to a man, made him aware of the gentling effect women exerted in an otherwise savage world.

Lorelei shifted, bit her lip, and replaced the goblet with another. "There. What do you think?"

I think I'd like to stretch this moment for a long while. Russell lifted the plate to assure himself he'd not been woolgathering and misheard the pattern name. "Virginia." Russell raised a teasing brow. "The silver is Mount Vernon. Are you going for a theme, here?"

"Of course," Lorelei set a pair of candlesticks nearby and crooked her head to examine the match. "You told me you were restoring the house. The patterns are old-fashioned looking and honor your heritage. Isn't that what you want?"

"I have the Hanover pattern," Mrs. Sweeny held out a plate with a touch of red amidst heavy gold embellishment around the edge. She cast a sideways glance at Lorelei, and her voice took on a decided bite. "It might suit your heritage, too."

Russell didn't like the undercurrent. He pushed to his feet and tucked Lorelei behind himself, as if to protect her from any cruelty. One ugly comment, and the peace he'd craved died instantly. Once again, he was a warrior, and he'd defend Buttercup from anyone who dared pose any threat or unkindness toward her.

"The lady already showed her preference. We'll just go elsewhere—"

"No! Oh, no, there's no need for that." Mrs. Sweeny blanched. "I misspoke."

"Yes, you did. Years ago, Americans didn't want my Irish ancestors to immigrate here. I went to war because our country believes all men are created equal." As he spoke, Lorelei shifted to stand beside him. His arm went about her waist, and he tucked her close to shelter her. "It would be unspeakable if the freedoms we fight for were denied the citizens at home."

"Yes. Of course you're right."

Russell dared to look at Lorelei. Her eyes glistened with tears, but instead of looking pained, she glowed.

"Russell, your words are so wise. Papa would have been so glad to know such a good man as you. For those things, he went to fight, too."

"We don't have to do business here."

Lorelei traced the tip of her forefinger on one of the cameo pictures on the salad plate. "Mrs. Sweeny is sorry. Even before America entered the war, her son's ship was hit by a German U-boat."

Lorelei obviously didn't want to make a scene, and Russell knew it would be best to follow her lead. He bought the china and led her out of the china shop, silently vowing he'd never spend another cent there.

As they waited at the corner for a buggy to pass before they crossed the street, Lorelei turned her face toward the sunshine. The joy on her face sent pangs of envy through him.

"Is there some specific charitable cause I should know about at the next store?"

Lorelei spluttered, then laughed. "Russell, even when you are wry, your wit tickles me."

He smiled back at her. She made being grumpy seem so ridiculously selfish. Few were the people he knew who could laugh at themselves; Lorelei did so regularly. She also coaxed him out of being in a bad mood simply with her sunny disposition.

They'd dropped her mother off at the mercantile in the first place. While they'd taken care of the other matters, Mrs. Goetz was supposed to arrange for several other items. Now Lorelei and her mother chattered like birds on a clothesline, and Lorelei kept insisting that Russell make a decision between two things. Finally, he leaned back against the counter and folded his arms across his chest.

"This must be done today so the house is ready for your guests," Lorelei scolded playfully.

Russell turned to Mr. Sanders. "I've got dozens of rooms to furnish, and she's fussing like I wouldn't have someplace to stick another bedstead. Just take all of the stuff and dump it in my buckboard. If it won't fit, deliver it."

"But you didn't decide on the material!" Lorelei's mother glowered at him.

He gave Mr. Saunders a yet-another-tempest-in-a-teacup look. The storekeeper grinned as Russell said, "Just throw the whole bolt of whatever fabrics she liked on there, too. Now give me a bottle of Bayer Aspirin. Domestic matters are a headache."

❧

Lorelei waited until they reached the mansion and started to unload the wagon. Mama had taken an armful of goods into the house before she tapped Russell on the shoulder. He turned around, holding a gleaming teakettle.

"What?"

"Your headache—is it all you have? Is anything else bothering you? In Boston, the navy is having many cases of the grippe."

"I heard about that. They're calling it the Spanish Influenza. You don't need to fret. I'm fine. Besides, there haven't been any cases down here or out west, so you can stop worrying."

A heavily laden wagon trundled up, and a young man jumped down. "Mr. Sanders ordered me to help carry all of this in. Where do you want it all?"

For the next two days, Lorelei and her mother went up to Russell's house. Russell was more than generous each time they worked for him, and the sock with their savings finally bulged.

Lace curtains hung in the parlor, and Mama had sewn new cushions for the window seat. She salvaged the material on the underside of the cushions and made pillows that still matched the old settee they'd uncovered. Russell had already stripped the wallpaper and freshly stained the floor, so he painted the walls a creamy color and nodded appreciatively as Lorelei filled the Heisey crystal vase with a fistful of black-eyed Susans.

She'd concentrated on the bedrooms. He'd painted each of them a pale shade of green. An ornate, white, wrought-iron bedstead in one room was covered with a deep green counterpane. It took very little time for Lorelei to stitch hems in dark green material, and after she hung the draperies, she pulled them open with white, tasseled cords. The room had no bedside table, so she tossed a tablecloth over a barrel and set a flowery, globed lantern on it.

The other room boasted cabbage rose bedding and curtains, and fresh, fluffy towels graced the washroom bars.

"What do you think of this?" Russell knocked on the top of a small chest of drawers. "I'm finding stuff in the attic that looks salvageable. When I first got here, I didn't bother, but since I'm going to need some furnishings, that place is full of stuff."

"That will be nice. Can you sand and stain it, or would it be easier to paint it white?"

"The grain's nice. I'll stain it. There are a few washstands and eight or nine chairs up there I'll bring down and either stain or paint."

"Your mother and sister—do they come from far away?"

He straightened suddenly. "Buttonhole. They live in Buttonhole."

"I am sure they will be very glad to see you." She gestured in a wide arc. "When they see all you have done—"

"That's the idea," he said curtly.

Lorelei quietly studied him, then asked, "Do you believe they will be so busy looking at your house that they will not see the trouble in your eyes and heart?"

fourteen

Russell's face hardened, and he gave no reply other than to turn and carry the piece down the stairs, off to the empty ballroom he used as his workshop.

Lorelei sat down at the top of the stairs. *Heavenly Father, Your voice holds together the universe. Please speak in a way that will soothe Russell's hurting soul. I dared to hope he'd been improving, but I was wrong. The changes were only on the outside, while inside he's so very broken. You, God—only You can heal the hurt he carries.*

❧

"You're Diamond?" A purser from the railroad scuttled up to Russell.

"Yes." Russell kept searching the trickle of folks disembarking.

"I was asked to give you this message. The phone and telegraph line to Buttonhole blew over in the gale, and the new one's not working."

Russell accepted the envelope and ripped it open. Just seeing his father's strong script brought back memories:

Dear Russell,
  Your mother and sister have both come down with a fever and are staying home. Mom says not to worry, that she'll come next week. She's missed you sorely, as have I. She complains your letters are too short. I would complain, too, but I'm no better, as you can see from this. We pray for you daily and trust the Lord to give you strength and peace.

  Love,
  Dad

P.S. We've sent some furniture to you. It once belonged in your house, and we wanted you to have these pieces.

Russell had dreaded seeing his mother, knowing full well Lorelei was right. Mom was far too perceptive to be deceived by a pretty bedroom and fragrant soap. She'd admire them, enjoy them, but she'd fuss over his leg and fret over how he'd changed.

What was a man to do? He'd gone to war with high ideals and heroic plans. He'd believed in God and country—well, country was still here, but where was God? Where was He when men all around were dying? The first day out, Jonesy—Russell's childhood friend—stood up and crumpled back into the trench, dead from a sniper's bullet. Men he considered brothers died all around him.

The very first man Russell killed had a rosary spill from his pocket. He'd undoubtedly thought God was with him, too. From that day on, Russell didn't open the Bible Dad had given him right before he left.

That had been the first of many lives Russell took. Kill or be killed—it was the most basic rule of warfare. The Bible said God created man in His image, and man was nothing but a bloodthirsty, cruel animal.

Mom and Dad lived such innocent lives. Their world was simple, their faith unshaken. Russell couldn't bear to look them in the eye and let them see what he'd become. Body, mind, and soul, he'd come home battered in ways no one would ever comprehend.

One more week of respite. . .but at what cost? Is Mom really all right? And Sis? Is it the Spanish Flu?

"Sir? Mr. Diamond." The purser scowled at him. "You need to claim your crates and sign for them."

"Sure. Fine."

He'd cleaned up an old buggy from the stable to come claim Sis and Mom. Clearly, he'd never manage the furniture. Russell arranged with the livery to deliver the large crates.

The house felt eerily empty when he got home. Once the oak secretary, rocking chair, and hall tree were in place, the feeling of loneliness intensified. Dad often sat at the secretary, going over order forms. Mom loved the rocking chair. The hall tree had no umbrellas, hats, or jackets on it to give it a homey air. As far as companionship, Mutt usually was all Russell wanted or needed, but tonight, he felt alone.

Russell couldn't sleep. He worried about his mom and sister. Had Dad taken sick, too? Russell purposefully didn't read magazines or newspapers because the major features were all about the war. Even so, he'd overheard stories about the influenza up in Boston. It killed strapping, healthy soldiers.

Did I tell Mom I loved her before I left?

❧

"Hop in. I'm going to town to make a telephone call."

Lorelei took hold of Russell's hand and nimbly climbed into the buggy. "Telephones are amazing, aren't they? Hearing a voice over wires—it doesn't seem possible."

"My dad had one put in his emporium. I always thought it was a nuisance because whenever anyone called, it fell to me to answer it and take messages."

Lorelei chuckled. "So now, who will have to take the message?"

"I'm calling my dad. Mom didn't come yesterday. She and my sister are both sick."

Lorelei twisted on the seat to face him. "Oh, Russell, I am so sorry to hear this. I will have to pray for them."

"You do that, Buttercup." His voice sounded grim, and he said nothing more the rest of the way to town. As soon as they entered the mercantile, Russell beelined to the telephone on the rear wall.

Lorelei decided to buy ten-pound bags of flour and sugar instead of five pounds since she'd have a ride home and she and Mama hadn't bought any for themselves in awhile. Then, too, she asked for a dozen brown eggs. Folks chatted and jabbered as usual. One of Mrs. Sweeny's sons had received a battlefield promotion.

After he finished his phone call, Russell prowled around the farthest aisles of the store. Noting his dark expression, Lorelei ventured over to him.

"How is your mother?"

"Dad said it's a nasty cold—nothing more." He didn't meet her eyes. "While I'm in town, I want to stock up. It'll take time. Is that a problem?"

"Not at all." She laughed. "With the unexpected ride, I'll still get home sooner."

By the time they left, Lorelei knew for certain they couldn't have wedged one more thing in the buggy. As it was, she held a crate on her lap that contained the oddest assortment of canned food she'd ever beheld. "Your larder will be full for at least a year with all of this."

"Don't blame me." He fished a can of chipped beef from the crate and toggled it in the air. "Mutt's the hungry one."

"She is by your side all of the time. How did you make her stay home?"

"It wasn't easy. Listen, Mom sent apples from our orchard back home. I'll eat a few, but they'll mostly spoil. Can you and your mom use them?"

"But of course. Oh. . . I should have bought more canning jars."

"I'll get you some if you promise to make cinnamon applesauce."

Lorelei laughed. "This applesauce—"

"*Cinnamon* applesauce."

"This cinnamon applesauce—I suppose it is also for your very hungry dog?"

fifteen

Russell carried Lorelei's measly ten-pound bags of sugar and flour into the cottage, barged into the kitchen, and started opening cabinets. "Where do these go?"

"In the canisters, Silly." Lorelei put down the eggs and gave her mother a hug.

"You will stay for lunch." Mrs. Goetz made it more of an order than an invitation, but he'd been counting on that.

"I can't stay long, what with that stuff in the buggy. Let me help." He opened the pantry and scanned the shelves. *They hardly have anything on them.* He cleared his throat. "What do you want?"

"I want you to sit down," Mrs. Goetz said as she pulled out a chair.

"Yes." Lorelei's eyes sparkled with humor. "Having seen your roast, Mama is sure your cooking would give us stomachaches."

"I'm never going to hear the end of that roast, am I?"

Lorelei and her mother said in unison, "No."

At dusk, they stood side by side and said the same thing. "No, Russell."

He rotated his shoulders, but the action didn't relieve the stress. As soon as he'd finished lunch, he'd driven the buggy to his back door, unloaded the contents, then changed his socks to the ones Mrs. Molstead had knitted. He unhitched the horses from the buggy and changed them over to the buckboard.

It took considerable fortitude to drive north to the Molstead's store. He did it for Lorelei, though.

Only Lorelei acted anything but pleased.

Russell folded his arms across his chest and glowered at the woman. "I didn't want to tell you this, but you're backing me into a corner. I have information that the flu is spreading."

"You don't read the newspaper, Russell." Lorelei made a dismissive gesture. "So far, they think it will stay up north. No one expects it to come down here, and experts say it will never go to San Francisco, either."

He'd hoped they'd simply accept what he told them. Clearly, Lorelei needed to be set straight. "You know I spoke with my dad on the telephone. He's got contacts all over because of the orders he places for his store. He said it's spreading—faster than folks realize. Dad's not one to panic, but he's not letting Mom or my sis come visit. That says plenty to me. After I spoke with him, I placed a few calls, myself."

"You truly are worried." Lorelei gave him a compassionate smile.

"I am." He didn't mince words. "You're going to have to cooperate with me, because the less often we go to town, the lower the chances are that we'll contract it."

"But influenza strikes the feeble, the old, and the very young," Mrs. Goetz reasoned.

"Not this one. People fifteen through forty are getting hit the worst." He hated scaring them, but he had no choice. "It's killing them in a matter of a day or two."

Russell didn't give the women a chance to demure. He hefted twenty-five pound bags of sugar and flour onto his shoulder and headed toward their kitchen door. Prices—especially of sugar—were high, so folks had been cutting back and buying smaller bags. He, on the other hand, was willing to pay top dollar, and the Molsteads gladly sold him as much as he wanted. Fatigue and the extra weight of the sacks made his limp worse. A sardonic smile twisted his mouth. His bum leg had provided a good excuse to buy several bottles of Aspirin.

Glass clinked behind him. Funny, how he'd come to associate Lorelei with that sound. "Russell," she said in her singsongy voice, "I hope you bought some cinnamon for the applesauce I'll put in these."

He shouldered the door open, dumped his burden near their pantry, and more than just the weight on his back lifted. He smiled at her. "Are four big tins enough?"

"Four!"

The shock in her voice still rang in Russell's mind as he crawled into bed that night. Exhausted as could be, he lay there and experienced the oddest sensation—security. He'd not felt this way since he went off to war. For the first time in ages, he'd been able to control matters and take action to make a difference.

The sickening knot in his stomach and the tension in his muscles eased as he closed his eyes and recalled his last glimpse of the Goetzes' kitchen. By the time he left, every last cabinet and shelf there bulged with provender. Astonishment and gratitude shone in Lorelei's eyes as she bid him sweet dreams as he walked past her toward the door. He rubbed his aching leg and let out a sigh. *She'll be safe now.*

❧

"All set." The iceman shut the door to the icebox and pulled a newspaper from his pocket. "Here's the paper. News is bad all over. The missus said to thank you for the pumpkins."

Mama handed him a burlap sack containing more bounty from their garden. "She is welcome. They grew well this year."

Lorelei sat on the new porch and opened the newspaper. Mama came out and settled on the chair. She started to shuck corn. "Read to me."

"Things look bad in the North," Lorelei said as she scanned the headlines. She didn't tell Mama about the article about another German store being vandalized.

"So Russell was right about the influenza?"

"Yes. Boston canceled its Liberty Bond parades and sporting events. In New York, they closed the theaters and symphony halls. The stock market is only open half-day. The influenza is awful in Europe, too. They've cancelled schools!"

"So terrible this is!"

Lorelei read aloud, and as she turned the page, Mama called out, "Good day, Russell!"

"How can you say it's good with what you're reading?" He waved his arm toward the newspaper.

Lorelei watched his gait as he approached. *He barely limps at all anymore. . .or is it just that I've grown accustomed to his walk? No. It is better, because on the days it pains him, I can tell by his bearing.*

"The day is beautiful, crisp, with the lovely autumn air and weak sunshine. The news is bad. Perhaps the church is doing something. We will see on Sunday."

"You can't be thinking of going to church!" Russell halted by the porch steps, leaned forward, and snatched the newspaper from Lorelei. "Public gatherings help spread the disease." He turned and appealed to Mrs. Goetz. "You've lost your husband; you can't possibly endanger your daughter!"

Lorelei folded her arms in her lap. *Dear Lord, let this be an opening.* "Will you make a deal with us, Russell? If we do not go to town for church, will you come to our house and worship with us?"

"Is that what it'll take?"

Lorelei glanced back at Mama, saw her nod, and turned back to him. "We would be pleased."

"Fine. Sunday." He stomped off.

"You know, it will be hard for him," Mama said softly. "He knows the Bible, but his faith is faltering."

"I know. He got angry when I was singing, 'Great Is Thy Faithfulness' out in the garden last week. He's still a soldier, but the battlefield is his soul."

"The Holy Ghost is wooing him. Maybe God will make something good happen out of all of this bad."

"With God, all things are possible." Lorelei scooted backward and reached up. Her fingers closed around her mother's cornsilk-tassel-covered hand. "Let's pray, Mama."

❧

"What was I thinking?" Russell angrily opened a can of chipped beef and dumped it in a bowl for Mutt. Russell plopped the bowl on the floor for the dog and didn't worry about the gravy that slopped over the edge. Mutt would make short work of it. He twisted and threw the empty can into the wastepaper basket with total disgust. "What under the sun was I thinking to agree to that ridiculous proposition?"

I care about them. The truth nearly knocked him off his feet. It was dangerous to care. How many friends did he make on the battlefield, only to lose them? How often had he shared a cold, miserable trench with someone, only to see him die? *This flu—it's killing people. It could claim any of us.*

The safest thing is not grow attached. Even though she's freshly widowed, Mrs. Goetz has a pleasant outlook on life and a gentle warmth. As for Lorelei. . .

Russell didn't want to admit it to himself, but the truth glared at him. He yanked out a chair and dropped into it. *She has a way about her—a compassion and joy for living that lights the dark corners of my heart. It's too late for me to keep from caring. I'll be sure to keep as much distance as possible.*

Really, it wouldn't be all that hard. He'd been essentially solitary since he'd arrived. Other than interacting with the workmen as necessary, Russell made a point of not socializing. All he'd do was walk down to the cottage for an hour or so on Sunday mornings, then ignore his neighbors the rest of the week.

Satisfied with that decision, he stood and tugged open a cupboard door. Scanning the cans of food, Russell felt a twist of disgust. Overseas, he'd eaten out of tins for months and promised himself he'd never eat out of them once he got home. Now that he was home, it didn't matter. Nothing tasted good. For the most part, he ate only because hunger forced him to. The meals Lorelei and her mother made were the exception. Russell couldn't figure out why he suddenly developed a decent appetite and appreciated the flavor of their food. He grabbed a can of tuna and wrinkled his nose as he opened it. It occurred to him that anything he didn't have to fix or something fresh ought rightfully be more appealing. *But when I've eaten at the diner, that might as well have been sawdust.*

He peeled off the lid and didn't bother to drain the can or mix it with anything. Hunched over the counter, he scooped out bites and shoveled them into his mouth.

Why did I agree to worship with them? I left the battlefield in France, but I'm still at war—only this is a personal war. I'm fighting with my soul, with God. Tradition and convention aren't good enough, and I'm not going to pretend.

Russell spent a sleepless night and a hectic day. He tried to find something to take his mind off the fact that he'd gotten roped into Sunday worship. Mucking out the stable and grooming both horses, raking and burning leaves—the heavy physical labor didn't distract him in the least.

The library beckoned—the one room he'd left entirely alone. Heavy draperies blocked out the sunlight, and sailcloth drooped in forlorn, dusty shrouds over the bookcases. Methodically, he removed and folded each piece of sailcloth from the outside to the middle, effectively capturing the worst of the dust. Whoever had closed up the house had taken great pains to try to preserve the books. Russell finally stretched his back and wiped his hands on the thighs of his jeans. He'd gotten a lot done—even if he'd been thinking of Lorelei all the while.

The next morning, he grudgingly put on a tie and walked to the cottage. Mutt trotted alongside him, and he figured it would be all right. *She'll probably behave better than I will.*

Lorelei opened the door, and a combination of aromas from the kitchen and her light, floral perfume greeted him. Her eyes sparkled. "We waited breakfast on you. There's even some applesauce—cinnamon applesauce."

He cracked a grim smile. They'd tried to do their part to make this comfortable. After breakfast, they moved from the kitchen table to the small parlor.

Lorelei smoothed her Sunday-best dress. "I thought to have us sing a bit, read a passage of Scripture, and pray."

Russell shuffled his feet and cleared his throat. "Ladies, I'll not be a hypocrite. I won't sing the words to those hymns. I don't feel them, and a man ought not misrepresent himself to the Lord or to others."

Mrs. Goetz smoothly invited, "Then listen and hum. You can appreciate the music, even if the lyrics don't quite match your thoughts."

Satisfied with that compromise, Russell sat down and hummed old, familiar hymns. Lorelei lovingly opened her Bible and paused a moment as she fingered the ribbon marking the passages she'd selected. She didn't start reading from the left page where the Psalms began. Instead, she shifted the Bible slightly and began reading. "Psalm four. 'Hear me when I call, O God of my righteousness: thou hast enlarged me when I was in distress; have mercy upon me, and hear my prayer. . .'"

Three psalms she read, her expressive voice rising and falling, carrying a range of emotions that made the psalmist come alive. Before now, the Psalms had never been much more than pretty words to Russell. The depth and complexity in the verses struck several nerves.

After Lorelei finished reading, Mrs. Goetz prayed. Lorelei once told him that her mother usually prayed in German, but at the meals they'd shared, she prayed in English. Even so, then, as today, she occasionally slipped and called God *Vater* instead of *Father*. Her prayer, so honest and intimate, made the ache in his heart double.

Seconds after saying, "Amen," Mrs. Goetz smiled at him. "Russell, you will stay for dinner?"

"I can't. I have to go." He stood and saw the surprise, shock, and chagrin on Lorelei's face. He couldn't help it. He had to get out of there, shift his thinking, and shut down the unexpected flood of emotions he felt from hearing David's words, the hymns, and prayer.

At home, the haunting passages played through his mind. He'd never appreciated how David was a warrior. He'd been besieged, seen comrades fall. *I will both lay me down in peace, and sleep: for thou, LORD, only makest me dwell in safety. . . .* The words from the psalm nagged him, taunted and wouldn't let go. Even after enduring combat, killing and seeing his own men perish, David could lie down in peace—and he slept. *Oh, to have my head hit the pillow and not relive the horror of what I saw and did!*

David the soldier was also David the musician, the one who sang unto the Lord. *I can't sing. Nothing flows from me but anger and sadness. How did David manage?*

As the week went by, Russell found himself humming as the words of hymns Lorelei and her mother sang seeped into his memory. *"Abide with me! Fast falls the eventide. The darkness deepens. . ."* Russell knew all about darkness—not just the pitch black of night, but of the ugliness of the soul. In the silent moments when Russell paused from his work to rub his leg or catch his breath, he'd recall the lyrics again and again. *"Lord, with me abide. . . ."*

The next Sunday, he took a harmonica to worship, hoping to drown out the lyrics. He didn't want to remember how he'd once treasured those hymns and believed them, had held faith in a loving God. Russell hoped if he concentrated on playing, the lyrics wouldn't continually intrude upon his conscience, but nothing could drown out the sweet blend of Lorelei and her mother's voices as they worshiped the God they loved so dearly—the same one who turned His face away and allowed Russell to wallow in the aftermath of man's ultimate evil.

No matter how hard he worked, regardless of the physical difficulty or the mental acuity required for a task, Russell couldn't free himself from the persistent reminders and memories of what Lorelei and her mother sang, read, or said. Between the songs of reverence and praise and the Scriptures, he left the Goetz cottage and lived with the echoes of worship all week long.

Daytime was hard enough; nights grew nearly impossible. Russell would lie in bed and fight to find a comfortable position. His leg troubled him after the exertions of the day, and that pain only compounded his inability to sleep well. He'd toss and turn, besieged by flashes of battlefield memories. Jolting awake, he'd struggle to reorient himself. In the moments after he established that he was safe in his bed, he'd try to substitute a different vision in his mind. Time and again, his thoughts would go to Lorelei as she held up a stained-glass window of Christ or as she read her Bible. Lorelei laughing. Sun shimmering on her golden hair as she bowed her head in prayer. She had the peace he craved. It didn't take a genius to figure out her peace ran soul deep—but the problem was, his trouble plumbed the depths of his soul.

Each Sunday, he kept his promise and went to their cottage.

At first, it was just to keep them safe, but in the following weeks it became a habit. Sunday morning became the only way he marked time. He'd left home and family behind in search of a refuge, to get away from others; yet, he paid a weekly visit to his neighbors, sat in their parlor, and examined how others in the Bible endured the separation from God he experienced.

Most of all, Russell identified with David. He'd lost his friend, Jonathan. He'd gone to battle, been brave, then shook with fear. Psalm after psalm revealed the ups and downs he'd experienced—the joys, the sorrows, the fears, the depression. David was just as likely to cry in grief and sorrow as he was to sing in victory.

David—David had known the ugliness that lurked not only in other men's souls, but in his own, too. War forced Russell to do things he'd never imagined himself doing. He'd slain—even rejoiced and taken pride in causing his enemies' deaths. That fact plagued him. . .but King David—the warrior, the psalmist—had done the same thing. And Lorelei said David was a man after God's heart.

Right and wrong—they once were so clear. Now, Russell struggled to reconcile a loving God with all He allowed to happen. As time passed, Russell's anger started to give way to unspeakable sorrow.

David had times of darkness when he couldn't see God's face. Why had he still called out to God? *And why can't I?* Russell shook his head. *I can't.*

sixteen

"It's cold in here."

Lorelei nodded absently and tapped a nail into the surface to keep the next piece of glass in place.

"Why didn't you light the fire?" Russell tromped across the workroom toward the potbelly stove.

"Please, don't light it." She looked over her shoulder at him. "The newspaper says it is best to leave the house cold. They think it kills the microorganisms for the influenza."

"The cold will kill you before it kills the germs. You don't dare catch a chill. It'll weaken your lungs and make you a prime target." He opened the grated front of the small stove, then slammed it shut.

"Come look at this window. I've been working on it for your parlor. Remember the pieces I couldn't match? I've removed the original edge, cut and used those pieces, and reformed the border with this opalescent gold. See how the amber makes the vertical lines shimmer?"

"What about that spot in the middle?"

"I couldn't quite make the glass stretch far enough, so I decided we'd put jewels here, here, and there." She touched the empty spots.

"Jewels?"

"Yes." She pulled a box from a shelf off to her right and opened the lid.

"Oh. Bauble things."

She laughed. "There are plain, smooth round ones, or we can use faceted ones. What do you prefer?"

He reached over her shoulder and used his forefinger to push the jewels around in the box until he found one that appealed to him. "This kind." He picked it up and set it on her work board. "Yeah. I like that a lot."

"I agree. We need two more." Before he could respond, Lorelei hurriedly added, "In fact, there are many supplies I need to buy—more lead cames, more solder, and emery so I can smooth out the chips on some of your pieces in order to repair them best."

"Make a list. I'll go to town."

"I knew you'd offer, but it won't work. I need to look at the things and decide for myself." She could see the fire in his eyes, so she hastily added, "If I'm to stay out of town, at least I should have the things necessary to keep myself busy."

"Don't you understand?" Russell glowered at her. "My mother and sister just had a simple cold and fever. Even after they recovered, they stayed in Buttonhole because by then, Dad wouldn't let them get on the train. It's utter foolishness to mix with people."

"I'm getting essentials, not going to a party."

"Lo-ri!" The frantic pitch of Mama's voice sounded from the house.

"Coming, Mama!" She started toward the house, and Russell rushed alongside her. "What is it?"

"We need to go check on Russell. Mutt is here. Perhaps something is wrong."

"Nothing's wrong, Mrs. Goetz." Russell brushed past Lorelei.

Her mother threw her arms around him and burst into tears. "I was so worried for you!"

"Shh," he murmured. Lorelei watched as he awkwardly embraced Mama. Seeing Mama's stark fear and how his tender nature surfaced touched her deeply. After a few minutes, Mama calmed down, and he announced, "Enough of this.

I'm worried about the two of you, and you're worried about me. My cooking is so bad, I'm likely to kill myself with something I fix. I'm moving you into my house."

"You can't mean it." Lorelei stared at him in shock.

Crafty as a fox, he ignored her and spoke to Mama. "Lorelei can share my workroom downstairs to do the windows. It will make it easier than creating them here and moving them."

"This would be good."

Lorelei slipped an errant hairpin back into place. "I can't finish this window or start on more until I have my supplies."

❧

Lost the battle, won the war. Russell shot Lorelei a surreptitious look as he drove the buckboard toward town. Her mother stayed home to pack up their necessary belongings. "This is a short trip."

"You've said that twice since we left home."

"I mean it." As they reached the edge of town, Russell felt her stiffen. "What is it?"

"The cemetery."

He leaned forward to look past her. Perfectly manicured grass normally graced the lot, but now it was pockmarked with multiple new graves.

"Mrs. Sweeny has black crepe on her door, but the stars on her flag are still white." Lorelei grabbed his arm. "Everyone is wearing masks."

Russell grimly hitched the horses outside the mercantile. "Stay put, and don't visit with anyone." He tied a bandana over the lower portion of his face and went inside. Moments later, he emerged with an entire bolt of cotton gauze. Hastily, he hacked at it with his pocketknife and folded the freed portion into a mask that he secured over her nose and mouth.

"Russell, look around us. There are posters in the windows,

warning of contagion and how to battle it."

"It's bad, Buttercup." He squeezed her hand. "Give me the list. I'll leave it with Mr. Saunders. He'll fill the order while we take care of everything else. I want to get out of here as quickly as possible."

At the hardware store, they found everything they needed for her windows and the repairs Russell was making. The china shop was closed, and a black wreath hung from the door. Lorelei's eyes filled with tears. "I used to walk down the street and see the star flags in the window. Now, there is black crepe everywhere."

Just then, a wagon started down the street. Two plain pine caskets rattled on it, and Mr. Sweeny sat in the back with them as the preacher drove the team.

"What time does the funeral start?" Lorelei asked in a subdued voice.

The pastor shook his head. "New orders are out. Family only. No church services—only fifteen-minute graveside commitments."

Russell reached around and tugged Lorelei into the lee of his body. He could feel her shaking. "We'll go home now."

"No, Russell. We must help."

He knew that look in her eye and the streak of stubbornness that ran straight through her. Instead of arguing, Russell let out a sigh. He searched for something that would satisfy her without putting her in danger.

"Tell you what, Buttercup. We'll go to the butcher and the mercantile. I'll load up and buy the biggest kettle they have and every last canning jar. You and your mother can bake bread and make soup. I'll bring it to town."

❧

"Here you go." Mrs. Goetz set one last paper-wrapped bundle in the bed of the buckboard. Flour streaked her apron, and she tried to brush it off. "You're starting out late today. The sun is setting earlier, too. If it gets too late, unhitch the wagon and ride home. The horses know the way."

"You go on in and rest. You're working too hard."

"Broth and bread are easy to make."

"You've made plenty of both for the past two weeks."

She pressed her hand to the bib of her apron. "In my heart, I make many more prayers than any loaves of bread. I pray God keeps you safe, Russell."

He reached town and took the list of homes from the light post. The pastor arranged to hang a roster from a string he'd knotted around the post, telling Russell which families needed bread and soup. He'd drop off the food on their porches and pick up the jars from the previous day.

Each day the list grew longer. Russell worked his way across town from one street to the next. Folks didn't stop to visit—they scurried away, eyes big with fear above the ever-present gauze masks. At the last stop, Russell walked up to the door. To his surprise, little Arnie was sitting on the stoop. The five year old had been the first in his family to come down sick. He'd only gotten out of bed two days ago.

"Arnie, it's late for you to be up."

Arnie looked up, and Russell's heart skipped several beats. The little boy's face was ashen, and his eyes huge. Dried tear runnels etched his cheeks. "Mommy won't wake up."

Russell knocked, then invited himself inside. A quick check revealed the worst: Both of Arnie's parents and his baby sister were dead. It would be foolish to take anything out of the diseased home, so Russell took off his shirt, wrapped the little boy in it, and headed toward the parsonage.

The pastor took one look at Arnie and bowed his head in grief. He paused a moment, then motioned Russell inside.

"No one's left at his house." Russell chose his words carefully as he lowered the child onto the couch. Arnie wouldn't let go of him, though, so he sat on the horsehair-stuffed cushion and kept the boy in his lap. "What about the rest of his family?"

The pastor wearily rubbed his forehead and sat in a nearby chair. "They've already passed on. He doesn't have anyone. All the families who were able to help out are overburdened. I can't see any choice. Arnie will need to go to Tepfield."

"Tepfield?" Russell gave the parson an appalled look. An orphanage was never a good arrangement, but in the midst of the epidemic, it would amount to cruel neglect at the best and death at the worst. Over in France, Russell hated seeing the ragged orphans wandering about hungry, frightened, alone. He refused to resign an American child to that fate. He took a deep breath. "I'll take him."

"Do you know the way?"

Russell shook his head. "No, I meant, I'll take him home with me."

"Praise be to God!"

Russell rose. "It's not temporary. I won't have him relocated later. He's been through enough."

"I agree." As the pastor led them back outside, he offered, "I'll handle the arrangements so you'll be assigned as his guardian."

Russell nodded. The commitment he'd just made ought to be staggering, but even amidst the sorrow surrounding the situation, the decision felt right. He set off for home. Along the way, Arnie snuggled in his lap. "That house has a star. Daddy says they have a boy in the war."

"Yes, they do."

Arnie pointed out house after house, mentioning the star flags. "There's a lellow star at that house. That means they gave a son."

Russell wondered if Arnie understood what that meant. *So*

much death. So much heartache. Why, God? Why?

The horses walked slowly since it had grown dark. They went past an open field. Arnie pointed up at the sky. "Look. Lots of stars. God has lots of boys like me."

"Yes, He does."

Arnie nudged Russell's chin. "Lookie. A big lellow star. God gave a Son, too."

It was all Russell could do to keep from roaring in his agony. Instead, he tightened his hold on Arnie. "What if I take you home and let you be my boy now?"

seventeen

Please, Lord, bring him home. It's grown so late. Keep Russell healthy and safe. He's been through so much, Father. Show him Your mercy and grace. The sound of the buckboard and horses jolted her. *Thank You, Almighty Father!*

Lorelei raced out onto the veranda. "Russell!"

"I brought home a nice little fellow." Something about his tone and the sorrow in Russell's eyes made Lorelei's breath catch. "Arnie's going to be my boy now."

She reached up and accepted Arnie. Russell had sacrificed his shirt to bundle the small boy. "You look tired, Arnie. Let me carry you into the kitchen. I'll make you a nice, warm snack; then we can put you to bed."

Arnie clung to Russell while Lorelei spooned chicken noodle soup into him. Mama didn't bother filling the bathtub; the kitchen was warm, so she pumped water into the sink, added hot water from the stove's reservoir until it was just the right temperature, then sang quietly as she bathed the boy.

Lorelei went upstairs to set up the cot, and Russell called to her, "Put it in the little parlor off my bedroom so I can hear him during the night."

After she did as Russell requested, Lorelei came downstairs to catch Russell burning his shirt and Arnie's clothing. Neither of them said a word.

Mama came in with Arnie bundled in a towel. "Russell, our little boy needs to borrow one of your undershirts. Tomorrow, I will sew some handsome clothes for him."

"I seem to recall trunks up in the attic with old clothes in them." Russell stood and gently took Arnie from Mrs. Goetz. "I'll tuck him in tonight and search for stuff for him first thing in the morning."

A short while later, Lorelei and her mother went up to bed. They peeked in on Arnie. Russell sat on the settee by the sleeping child's cot, looking as if the weight of the world had fallen on his shoulders. Mutt lay curled at his feet.

"You look so domestic," Lorelei whispered.

He raked his fingers through his hair in agitation. "He doesn't have anyone. Pastor said there isn't anyone left in his whole family. I promised I'd watch over him, but I can't do it alone. I can keep him warm and fed, but I don't have the love and solace he'll need."

Lorelei opened her mouth to refute his words, but Mama silenced her with a touch and said, "We will help you. Arnie needs a whole family, and together, with God's loving help, we will become what he needs."

"I'll fix up this little room for him. He was afraid to be by himself."

"We can do that tomorrow. For now, let's all get some rest." Lorelei gently ruffled Arnie's hair and smoothed his blankets. "No fair going to the attic alone, Russell. I want to see what's stored up there."

He leaned his head back on the settee and said, "There's something else."

Lorelei dreaded what else might have gone wrong. *Lord, please don't let him have lost someone dear to him. He can't take it.*

"Buttonhole is almost decimated by the epidemic. I got a telegram from my dad. So far, you and I have done well by staying isolated, and I'm thinking about having my mom load up some of my cousins who are the most vulnerable and having them come to stay here."

"This is something to pray about," Mama said sagely.

"We'll go back to our cottage. You'll have plenty of room." Lorelei smiled at him.

He bolted upright. "No! I thought you just promised to help me with Arnie. I just wanted to know if you'd mind having more people underfoot."

"God blessed you with a mansion, Russell. I think it would be a sin to leave rooms empty when they could harbor children who need a safe place."

"I'll think on it more tonight."

"And we'll pray," Mama said. She shook her finger at Russell. "I get to look in that attic tomorrow, too. If we are going to fix up more bedrooms, I might find things up there we can use."

❧

"Look at these!" Lorelei dusted off a pair of pineapple-topped bedsteads. "They'd be wonderful together in one of the larger bedrooms. It is odd, though, these pineapples."

"They're an old American symbol of welcome," Russell said absently as he lifted an old ceramic chamber pot.

Arnie, who clung to Russell's leg announced, "I don't got one of those under my new bed."

"Then it must be yours." Russell chuckled.

Lorelei knelt and smoothed her hand over another piece of wood. "What is an altar doing up here?"

"Family lore is, the church burned down the night one of my ancestors proposed. He ran into the church and saved the altar for his bride's sake. He knew she'd want it for their wedding."

"Yes. Yes, I believe this. Part of it is burned."

Mama bent over a trunk that was pressed way beneath the eaves. "The top of this had had much rain, but inside, it looks good. There are clothes here—old ones that belonged to a woman." She dug deeper. "Oh, bless the Lord! There are clothes here for a little boy!"

"Count your many blessings," Lorelei started to sing.

"Mommy sings that song to me. When is Mommy going to come get me?"

Russell sat on the floor of the attic and tugged Arnie around so the boy stood eye-to-eye with him. "Mommy was very sick. Daddy, too."

"And Baby 'Liz'beth."

"They died, Arnie. Do you know what that means?"

Lorelei knelt on the floor and said, "It means they sleep in heaven now with Jesus."

Arnie's eyes filled up with tears. "But what 'bout me?"

"You're going to sleep in your new room here," Russell said. "You're going to be my boy now."

The little boy's face puckered. "Am I 'posed to put lellow stars in the window?"

Mama came over and opened her hand. Three golden buttons in the shape of stars lay nestled in her palm. "Better than that, Sweetheart. You'll wear the yellow stars."

ஐ

"I'm going." Lorelei set down her soldering iron so hard, the pieces of glass jumped. The room that had once been an enormous parlor and ballroom rang with her words.

"Don't be so stubborn. It's for your own good."

"You are my friend, not my father," she said hotly. "You cannot make me go to my room like a naughty child." *Even if you want to. . .*

"See reason."

"I am seeing reason. It will be necessary to get essentials."

"For crying in a bucket, Lorelei, I'm losing my patience. I have enough china and silver to feed an army."

"But you do not have towels enough nor sheets. You don't even have mattresses for the beds! I know what to get; you do not. Of course I should go to town."

He stared at her. "I tell you what: My dad and mom own a mercantile. You make a list, and I'll have them fill a freight wagon. I'd rather have them ride here than come by train, anyway."

Jaw clenched to the point that the tiny muscles on the side of his cheek twitched, he bent over a little chest of drawers and resumed sanding it with long, heavy strokes. The grating *swish* against the sudden hush in the room sounded unnaturally loud.

The patter of little feet echoed on the marble entryway, giving warning that Arnie had awakened from his nap and would be with them in an instant. The little boy burst into the workroom and zoomed toward Russell. "There you are. I thought you were gone."

Russell let go of the sandpaper, knelt, and opened his arms wide. Arnie ran straight to him and hung on tight. His eyes and voice were filled with tears, "Don't leave me."

"Leave you?" Russell pulled away and gave the little boy a playful shake as he repeated in a voice full of patently mock outrage, *"Leave you?* Do you know what I've been doing this morning while you slept in?"

Arnie shook his head.

Russell thumped his palm on the top of the chest of drawers. "I was fixing this for your bedroom. You'll need it to hold the clothes Mrs. Goetz found for you."

Arnie stood on tiptoe and stared at the compact wooden piece. "What're you doing to it?"

"I didn't want you to get any splinters, so I'm sanding it."

"Can I help?"

Lorelei watched as Russell opened his arms and heart to Arnie. It came as such a surprise. He was normally so standoffish—but there he was, a tall, broad-shouldered, gruff man with a tattered-looking mutt on one side and an orphaned little boy on the other.

He'll make a good father.

The thought sent streaks of warmth through her. *Deep inside Russell, there is tenderness and goodness. Surely, there must be hope for him.* She pensively brushed flux on the joints she needed to solder. *Jesus, You are the lover of our souls. Please, shower Your love on this man. Wash away the pain and doubts, and allow his spirit to flourish again.*

"Are you thinking about what to put on the list?" Russell's words made her look up. "I'll need to go place the telephone call this afternoon. While I'm there, I'll deliver the soup and bread and can pick up a few of the smaller things at the mercantile."

"You'll wear a mask the whole time?"

He nodded.

"Me, too." Arnie bobbed his head, a miniature replica of Russell.

Lorelei gave Russell a startled look. He wouldn't let her go to town; he couldn't possibly allow Arnie to. In those tense seconds, Arnie's eyes widened, and he grabbed a fistful of Russell's pant leg.

"Hey, now, Buddy." Russell shifted and gave Lorelei a bail-me-out-of-this look.

"Russell doesn't want me to go to town, either." She came around the worktable and sighed. "I suppose we'll have to keep each other company and watch Mutt for him until he gets home tonight. In just a few days, some big, big boys and girls are coming to visit. We can surprise Russell with how much we get done on the bedrooms for them."

"It's about lunchtime." Russell ruffled Arnie's hair. "You can help us think of things our guests will need to bring."

"I didn't bring nothing."

"You most certainly did!" Lorelei laughed at Arnie. "You brought Russell back home in the dark!"

&

"Everybody's settled in for the night."

Russell didn't turn toward his mother's voice. Instead, he continued to stare out the bank of windows at the back of the house, out into the darkness where the sky and ocean met. Moon flecks on the water and stars in the sky make it almost impossible to tell them apart.

Lots of stars. God has lots of boys like me. Arnie's words kept echoing in his memory. *Lookie. A big lellow star. God gave a Son, too.*

"You have a beautiful view of the stars," Mom said as she stood beside him. She snuggled into his side. The top of her bun tickled his jaw, and she smelled like the peach soap he'd bought especially for her. "Thanks for inviting us to come, Honey. I've missed you so much. Your father sends his love."

He pressed a kiss on her temple. "You're tired, Mom. Go to bed."

"My room is lovely. Did Lorelei help you with it?"

Lorelei moved out of that very room and in with her mother. Still, Russell didn't want his mom playing matchmaker. "Lorelei and her mother did it together, just as they worked on the other bedrooms."

He'd managed to turn her around and walk her toward the entryway. She stopped and smiled. "The hall tree looks wonderful here."

"It does. Thanks for sending it. I want this mansion to look as much to period as I can make it."

"While we're here, the kids can help. Alan and Philip could help you paint and work outside—especially cut back some of the shrubs and pull out the dried weeds."

"I'll keep 'em busy."

"I brought bolts of fabric. I'll have the girls sew each day, and they can help in the kitchen."

"Mrs. Goetz will appreciate it. The town just started using the local dance hall as a makeshift hospital. Late each afternoon, I deliver soup and bread to it instead of going to individual homes as I used to."

"But is that safe?"

"It limits any exposure, and everyone has to help out." He took her arm and forced a chuckle as he escorted her up the stairs. "I can't believe you'd fret. I've spent my entire life watching you make baskets and deliver them to everyone in Buttonhole that had so much as a bruise, bump, or boil."

"Those aren't catching, Russell."

"Nothing's killed me yet." Once he said the bitter words, he regretted them—they were truthful, but he'd promised himself he'd shield his mother and cousins from the ugliness inside. They'd just arrived early this evening, and he'd already stepped far over the line.

eighteen

Lorelei smiled as she watched Mrs. Diamond organize her nieces. She'd sent the dark-haired one to the kitchen to help Mama make bread. "Beatrice, Beatrice," Lorelei chanted under her breath to remember who was who.

Three girls, two boys, and Russell's Mama made for quite an addition to the house. They ranged from thirteen to seventeen and all had the look of children setting out on a holiday adventure instead of ones hiding from a terrible epidemic.

"Lacey, I know you girls brought your sewing boxes. Go fetch them and bring them to the parlor. Adele, wipe down the dining table so there's nothing sticky left from breakfast. We'll use that as a cutting table."

Lacey is blond, and Adele is the youngest.

While the girls all scattered to do as they were bid, Mrs. Diamond walked over to Lorelei's worktable. "Oh, this window is lovely, just lovely. Where is it going?"

"In the smaller parlor, just on the other side of that wall."

"I'm surprised at how few windows needed to be replaced. After the house sat vacant for so long, I expected it to be a hideous mess."

"Russell has done considerable work. He's put on a new roof, painted the outside, replaced more than fifty panes of glass, rebuilt the veranda. . . ." She made a spiraling gesture. "So many more things, too. It used to look like a magnificent bridal gown that somehow ended up with torn lace, smudges of dirt and mud, and a sagging hem. Now when I look at the house, I see what the mansions in heaven must be like."

"Will you be doing any more stained glass for the house?"

Lorelei nodded. "Russell found an old photograph when he took the drawers out of one of the washstands. It showed that there used to be large, floral windows on either side of the front door. I'm to reproduce them, but first, he must decide on the colors. Perhaps you could help him."

"Evidently my son hasn't told you my embarrassing secret."

"Russell is discreet. He would not speak badly of anyone."

Mrs. Diamond picked up a little scrap of glass and held it up to the light. Her voice lilted with merriment. "I love pretty things, but when it comes to putting them together, I'm hopeless. Why, when my husband courted me, he actually had to point out that my clothing was ragged and faded as a beggar's."

"You cannot mean this!"

Mrs. Diamond laughed and nodded. "It's the absolute truth. In fact, I was hoping you'd help me look at the bolts of cloth we brought along so I can start the girls sewing some quilts and pillows or cushions for the rooms. That bedroom I'm in is utterly charming, so I know you have an eye for these things."

"The bedroom where Adele and Lacey sleep needs curtains. Perhaps that would be a good project to do first. I have the measurements of the windows, so that will make it easy."

Mrs. Diamond set down the piece of glass and nodded. "Wonderful idea. I'm sure they'll enjoy decorating their room. I want to keep the children busy so they'll not get into trouble or be too homesick."

"Russell once mentioned he has a list of things he wishes to do. Perhaps you could read it to see what might make good projects."

"Aunt Rose, do you know where Russell is?"

They turned toward the door. A younger version of Russell stood there, still at the gangly stage where he was all knees and elbows. His voice cracked midsentence as he added, "I found a bunch of paint in one of the stalls, and I was thinking we could spruce up the stable. Russell has a pair of geldings out there."

"Out exploring, Philip?"

"Yes." He shrugged. "This is a nifty old place. Russell must be having a great time, fixing it up."

Lorelei had seen Russell work. He wasn't having a great time at all—the work was demanding and pressed him to his limits. Nonetheless, he determinedly forged ahead. Sometimes, she watched him as he toiled, and she'd arrived at the conclusion that he pressed himself until exhaustion would allow him to sleep. Still, he slept poorly. Every single night, he groaned or shouted out in his dreams. Refusing to reveal any of those facts, Lorelei looked about the room and said, "He's put much care into this place."

Philip wandered across the floor and gawked around. "It was too dark to see much yesterday. My dad said he'd been by a couple years ago, and the place was nothing but a dirty wreck. He ordered me to test the floors to be sure they hadn't rotted, but I can see that's not necessary."

"Russell replaced the veranda here and the porch down at the cottage." Lorelei noted the envious gleam in Philip's eyes and added, "Russell mentioned some of the rooms in the attic sustained rain damage. If you are as skilled as Russell, you might wish to ask him if he could use your help in repairing them."

"Wow. Yeah. I'd like that. I brought some tools along—in case he needed that kind of help."

"You said my son has a list of projects?" Mrs. Diamond shot Lorelei a conspiratorial glance.

"Perhaps we could ask him to show it to us at lunch. Mama always told me a man is easier to deal with when his stomach is full."

Philip sniffed and grinned. "Smells like the bread is out of the oven. The kitchen is like a big city bakery—loaves and loaves all laid out and more dough, ready to bake."

Lorelei laughed. "Mama loves to cook. You should ask her about her cinnamon rolls. She would be happy to make you some."

"Really?"

Lacey, having entered the room with the sewing baskets, chimed in, "Cinnamon rolls?"

"Now I don't know. . . ." Russell's mother shook her head.

Lorelei laughed. "I'm sure. They're Mama's favorite, so it would give her a good excuse."

Russell called from the window, "What's going on in there, and why does someone need an excuse?"

≥≈

Lorelei rolled over and blinked at the shaft of sunlight creeping though the chink between the halves of her curtains. *Lord, it's Your day today. Russell isn't going to let anyone go to town. Will You please grant him some comfort as we worship here with the children?*

She yawned and burrowed beneath the quilt for a few more minutes, mentally going through a list of hymns they might sing. "Stand Up, Stand Up for Jesus, ye soldiers. . ." No, that wouldn't do. "Onward, Christian Soldiers. . ." Lorelei grimaced. She'd never noticed how many songs used words like *soldier* or *battle*.

Heavenly Father, help us to keep this day of worship holy and special. Let it unfold according to Your will, and make me sensitive to what You would have us say, do, sing, and read. Russell is hurting, and he needs Your healing touch. The children all miss their parents. Arnie clings to Russell, to Mama, and to me because he is so afraid of losing any of us. Tender Shepherd, we need Your touch and mercy. Guide and direct us I pray. Amen.

"You're awake, Lori?" Mama whispered.

"Yes, Mama."

"I dreamed of your papa reading the Bible to us. Remember how he smoothed the ribbon back into the pages when he was done?"

"Every time." The memory made sorrow wash over her.

"I was thinking about how I wished the ribbon on that Silver Star medal the government brought us for your Papa was smooth, deep blue satin instead of striped grosgrain." Mama rolled over. Tears glossed her eyes. "I decided to put blue satin in the box the medal came in."

Tears spilled down her cheeks as Lorelei reached over and pulled her into a tight hug. When she found her voice again, she whispered, "That's a nice idea, Mama."

A little while later, when they'd regained their composure, Mama sat on the bedside and combed her hair as she said, "Russell's mother tells me he got a medal, too—the same as your papa's."

"I'm not surprised. He's a man of honor and courage." Lorelei bent to tie her shoes and added quietly, "But I don't think we'd better ask him about his medal. He doesn't want to talk about the war."

"His eyes hold much hurt, Lori."

"So does his soul." She straightened. "Which makes me wonder, what shall we do for worship today?"

"I know just the right verses." Mama gave her a watery smile. "And Rose Diamond has a lovely voice. She can help us decide on some hymns."

They slipped downstairs, and Mama stirred up the fire she'd banked in the stove last night. Lorelei opened the kitchen door and pulled in the milk Mr. Rimmon delivered. Before the epidemic, he'd delivered a single half-gallon bottle to each house twice a week. Now, he left a half-full, tin, ten-gallon milk can each dawn. He'd already strained it and left half a gallon of cream, too, so they could churn their own butter.

"Hi!" Arnie skipped through the kitchen, accompanied by Mutt. Only a step behind, Russell nodded and turned the knob to let them out. The three of them were nearly inseparable, and Mama and Mrs. Diamond both thought it slightly scandalous that Russell allowed the dog to sleep at the foot of Arnie's bed, but no one dared interfere since the three of them seemed to need each other.

Soon the kitchen smelled of yeast from the bread dough and cinnamon from the rolls. Beatrice sat in a chair over by the window, using the Daisy paddlewheel churn. Mrs. Diamond had Adele setting the table as Lacey rearranged the parlor for "church." Alan and Philip went to muck out the stable. The routine in the household hadn't taken long to establish, and it carried with it a comfortable air. It didn't take much longer before everyone sat down to breakfast.

After the meal, Russell ordered the boys to carry their chairs to the parlor for worship. Everyone found a seat, and Mrs. Diamond led the singing. True to form, Russell didn't sing, but he played his harmonica.

෧

Russell lifted Arnie onto his lap to stop him from squirming as Mrs. Goetz started reading from the second chapter of Nehemiah.

> "Wherefore the king said unto me, Why is thy countenance sad, seeing thou art not sick? this is nothing else but sorrow of heart. Then I was very sore afraid, And said unto the king, Let the king live for ever: why should not my countenance be sad, when the city, the place of my fathers' sepulchres, lieth waste, and the gates thereof are consumed with fire? Then the king said unto me, For

what dost thou make request? So I prayed to the God of heaven. And I said unto the king, If it please the king, and if thy servant have found favour in thy sight, that thou wouldest send me unto Judah, unto the city of my fathers' sepulchres, that I may build it."

Russell stared at the worn Bible in her lap. He couldn't recall hearing that passage before now. *Sorrow of the heart. Yes, that said it well. And I'm also rebuilding what belonged to my ancestors. Nehemiah felt this way, too?*

"Russell is rebuilding." Adele smiled at him.

Arnie waved across the room at her, which seemed to serve better than the stingy smile he, himself, barely managed. *What am I doing with all of these tenderhearted children here?*

Alan cleared his throat. "I'm thinking of that verse about building a house. I don't recall where it is."

"The one about whether you build a house on rock or sand?"

"That's a nice one, but not the one that I had in mind. It's about laboring in vain if God isn't building the house."

Russell cleared his throat. "That's Psalm 127:1. 'Except the Lord build the house, they labour in vain that build it: except the Lord keep the city, the watchman waketh but in vain.'?"

Mom patted Alan on the arm. "Russell's mind is like a camera. He need see something only once, and he remembers it forever."

And there are things I wish I'd never seen and wouldn't remember. . . . He stared at the floor. The autumn sun streamed through the stained-glass window Lorelei had restored, and the golden segments she'd cleverly borrowed from the border and stretched to fit by using the amber jewels he chose ended up casting a golden cross on the far wall.

Lorelei suggested, "Let's finish with sentence prayers. Anyone who would like can join in."

The prayers and the glass-cast golden cross don't bother me, he realized with shock. When he'd first come back from France, those things would have set him on edge. Now, after weeks of quiet worship and hearing Lorelei read the Word of God aloud, he'd let go of most of his anger. At times, it still surged, but, for the most part, a profound emptiness replaced the rage.

Their faith is touching, innocent. I was like that once. A sense of loss swamped him. He held Arnie and rested his chin on the little boy's soft hair. Wrapping his arms tighter, he realized how much he wanted Arnie to grow up believing that Jesus loved him. Lorelei's sweet, husky voice chimed in with a word of prayer.

Russell's leg ached, but his heart ached more. *Even if I can't patch together my own faith, I want this little guy to have the assurance and security Lorelei has.*

❧

"Russell, I brought you your jacket." Lorelei knew she needed to speak before she approached him. He'd been lost in thought, and sudden sounds and movement always resulted in startling or angering him. The past week had been particularly bad. He'd been going to town and digging graves, coming home only to get the bread and soup, then returning again late in the evening. The bleakness in his eyes and the groans in his sleep bore testimony to the great cost of the work he'd done.

"The air, it is chilly much of the day now. It is good that we have so much wood piled up for the winter." Slowly, she walked across the veranda and out into the yard.

Russell pushed away from the tree and shrugged into his jacket. "Thanks."

"You are troubled."

"I'm not decent company, Lorelei. Go back inside."

An undertone of anguish in his voice made her stay. "I didn't ask if you were good company. If I wanted pleasant companions, there are plenty in the house."

"Are they getting under your skin?"

She laughed. "I just said they were pleasant companions, Russell. Your mother is a wonderful woman, and your cousins are delightful. My place is not with them right now; my place is to be with a friend who is hurting."

"Who's hurt?" He stiffened as he barked the question.

Lorelei paused a moment, then quietly answered, "You."

nineteen

Lord, I felt led to come out to Russell, but I feel so unsure of why You have me here. I have no understanding of the pain he feels or what to say to him.

"My leg's never going to get better." He snorted. "I'm going to limp for the rest of my life. The shrapnel left in there is too close to the nerves and arteries to mess with, so the ache's permanent. I'm a cripple. There. Did that clear the air?"

"The ache, this I am sorry for. The limp—it has gotten better over the months you have lived here. It does not keep you from doing the things you wish. Your body serves you well, Russell, and you use your strength and talents for others. I hold no pity for you, only gratitude. You have a battle raging inside you, yet you had the kindness and courage to think of others."

"Don't fool yourself. I came out here because I was thinking only of myself."

"You need time alone. What is wrong about that? There have been days when I sought solitude in my sorrow and confusion."

"Buttercup." His voice sounded ragged. She liked how he occasionally called her such a pretty name, even if he said it in a jaded tone. Somewhere deep inside, it meant that he still longed for good things, even if he denied himself.

"Yes?"

"I'm as splintered and jagged as the broken glass you sweep up. You don't know what you're dealing with."

"What I know is, even when glass is shattered, the pieces can be fit together in a new way to make something beautiful."

Russell shook his head. "Not me."

"You must be patient. Papa used to patiently fit the pieces of a window together. He refused to hurry. These things take time. He taught me that if something is to last, it must be tended with diligence now—whether it is a window or a soul."

"You still believe in fairy tales, Lorelei."

"I'm a grown woman, Russell. I didn't fight in a war, but I have lost my father, and I've worked hard to make a living and provide for my mother. I believe in God's love. I believe in family. I believe in friends. The pattern I envisioned for my life was shattered, but I chose to put the pieces back together. The picture is different, but the Source of my light never changed."

He smashed his fist into the trunk of the tree. "My friends died! Don't you get it? All around me, my friends bled and died. I used my rifle, my trench knife, even my bare hands and killed Germans—men who had families and friends back in their hometowns. I've seen slaughter, I've slain, and I'm sick to death of death."

Lorelei quietly reached over and curled her hand around his wrist. He yanked free, but she persisted and took his wrist again. Gently, she brushed bark off his skinned knuckles. "You are hurting enough on the inside, Russell. Don't hurt yourself on the outside, too."

"There's blood on my hands and in my soul." He pulled free.

"Only the Living Water can wash that away." She folded her arms around her ribs. "Once, I told you the red glass was the most expensive. Right now, the only color you see in the window of your soul is red. Christ already paid the price to purify it. Regardless of the color, though, know that I care for you as a friend. Your pain doesn't frighten me away."

&

Russell sat at the head of the supper table long after the meal was over and everyone had left the dining room. Arnie didn't want to leave his side, but Adele promised to teach him how to play checkers. Laughter and chatter drifted across the marble entryway and into the dining room. The swinging door to the kitchen sat ajar, allowing a wedge of light and the musical conversation between Lorelei and their mothers.

At the first lunch they all shared, Mom, Mrs. Goetz, and Lorelei had created a schedule of chores. They'd all insisted on taking a turn at dishes, too. Mom and Mrs. Goetz spent a couple hours each day in the library, clearing off bookshelves and oiling the wood. In another day or so, that room would be an inviting haven of peace.

The girls rotated into the kitchen for a day, then sewed for two. They hadn't decided on any particular room—they'd stitched in the parlor, in a bedroom, on the verandah—so no matter where he turned, Russell seemed to run into someone. Simple, gathered cotton curtains hung from the windows in the kitchen, bedrooms, and washroom, and the duvets in the girls' rooms bore new, matching covers. A lacy, tatted doily lay in the center of the dining table beneath the mum-filled Heisey crystal vase.

The boys eagerly traipsed through the house and over the estate, then voiced which projects appealed to them the most. After the first day, Russell decided he'd make assignments so he'd know where they were and what they were doing; finding Philip "fixing" the stairs to the attic reinforced the need for that decision.

So far, the washroom and four bedrooms sported fresh coats of paint, a wobbly chair's legs now measured even, and two doors that used to sag and stick were planed and rehung. The stable sported a fresh coat of barn red paint, and most of the shrubs had been cut back to manageable level. Once set to work, the boys did fairly well. Their exuberance sometimes eclipsed their judgment, but, overall, they hadn't been too much trouble.

How did I ever end up with this troop in my barracks? He stared at the hodgepodge of chairs about the table. Counting Lorelei, Mrs. Goetz, Arnie, his mother, and five cousins, he'd taken on responsibility for nine other people. *And to think I came here to get away from everyone.*

He let out a burdened sigh. His father hadn't asked him to take on these guests; he'd simply revealed how bad things were in Buttonhole and asked how Russell was doing since he lived so far on the outskirts of a town. Survival: the first rule of war—and they were fighting a deadly enemy in the form of an epidemic. Russell knew he'd made the right decision. It didn't make it any easier, though, when he craved solitude.

Suddenly, rifle fire split the night air.

"Sniper!" He dove out of his chair and crawled to the doorway. "Down! Down! Everybody down!"

His pulse thundered in his ears as feet pounded on the floor.

"Russell? What's wrong?"

Someone burst through the front door. Russell grabbed Lorelei and yanked her to the floor. She tumbled over him, and he shoved her into the corner where she'd be safest.

"Alan bagged a buck! Come see!"

Sweat poured down Russell's temples and tension made him jump as Lorelei gently rubbed his back. "A deer, Russell. Alan hunted a deer. In your yard in Virginia, Russell. You're home, not in the war."

A shudder rippled through him. It took another second or two to fully understand her. He bolted to his feet, yanked her upright, and strode as fast as his limp allowed him out to the front yard.

Alan stood over a buck on the far side of the hedges, chest thrust out and shoulders squared with pride. "How do you like this?"

Russell grabbed the rifle from him. "I don't."

"We'll have venison roast, and Mrs. Goetz can make stews for the folks in town."

"That's no excuse. None at all," Russell bit out. Memories of what a rifle shell could do to a human being burst through his memory, making his voice harsh. "In this light, you couldn't be sure what you were shooting. Do you understand me?"

"Hey, I was just trying—"

"No excuse," Russell repeated himself through gritted teeth. He stared at Philip. "If you have a weapon, you're to give it to me now. No one hunts without my permission."

Arnie started to sniffle. Lorelei stooped, pulled him into her arms, and rose. She patted his back and cooed, "It's okay, Honey. It's okay. He's not mad at you. Russell worried that someone got hurt because he cares about us."

"You children go back inside." His mother gave the order firmly. Spreading her arms wide, she herded them toward the house and didn't leave any chance for objections.

Alan stood belligerently over his kill. Russell's hand curled tighter around the stock of the rifle he'd carefully kept aimed at the ground. He stared at Alan until the teen looked away, then commanded, "This is your kill—you dress it."

"I. . .um. . .don't know how."

"Then it's time you learn."

"I could help." Lorelei's soft, husky voice startled Russell. He shot her a strained look. She set Arnie on the ground and gave his little backside a pat to send him on his way.

The last thing I need is for her to weaken my stance with the kids—if that's possible.

Russell shook his head. "This is Alan's mess. He's not a child, he's a young man. A responsible young man handles his own affairs."

≈

The next evening, Mama and Mrs. Diamond declared it was a

celebration night. All of the rooms on the second floor and the three maid's bedrooms in the attic were painted. The occupied rooms all had curtains; refurbished furniture; spreads, duvets, or quilts; and pictures. Beatrice had shown remarkable artistic flair, and her works hung here and there.

Mrs. Diamond fixed a big venison roast while Mama used breadcrumbs to make dressing. Lorelei passed the okra over Arnie's head to Russell and teased, "Now aren't you glad you gave us that garden?"

"He's more likely to be thankful there are a bunch of us at the table to eat the okra." Mrs. Diamond laughed. "Russell doesn't care for it."

Lorelei gaped at him.

He cleared his throat. "I'd like some of your beans, though. Between the corn and beans you canned, I'm still glad you garden."

Mrs. Diamond took the bowl of green beans from Philip and passed them to her son. "Like father, like son. Did Russell ever tell you I have a fruit orchard?"

Lorelei nodded. "He shared the apples you sent."

"Mom makes peach everything—jam, tarts, pies," Russell began.

"Don't forget her cobbler!" Philip tacked on.

"Yes, well, Russell's father had me fooled about liking peaches for the longest time. It wasn't until he asked me to marry him that he confessed he can't stand the taste of peaches!"

While others laughed, Lorelei felt a twang of worry. "Did you give me the apples because you don't like them? Is that why you want cinnamon in your applesauce—to hide the flavor?"

"Love them." Russell tipped his head to the side and gave her an assessing look. "That apple I'm smelling—it's not the cider you're drinking?"

Arnie piped up, "Nope! Lorelei made apple doodle. It's a s'prise."

"Strudel," Lorelei corrected softly as she saw the deliciously greedy spark in Russell's eyes.

"You told!" Arnie glared up at her. "Now it's not a s'prise."

After dessert, everyone played musical chairs in the entryway with Russell controlling the tunes on the gramophone, then everyone bundled up and went outside.

A big pile of leaves and logs lay ready. Russell supervised Alan as he lit it. Sugar prices made candy cost an arm and a leg; marshmallows were a rarity. The bag of marshmallows Russell's mother brought out to toast counted as the highlight of the whole evening.

"Uh-oh. I burned mine!" Arnie's face puckered.

"Yum! Just the way I like it!" Russell swiped the charred, gooey mess and popped it into his mouth. "I suppose you like them all golden perfect like Lorelei's, don't you Arnie?"

"Uhn-huh." The boy nodded.

"Shh. We have to be sneaky," Russell said in a stage whisper. He grabbed Lorelei's stick, and she obligingly let out a shriek.

"Lorelei, Russell has a marshmallow on his stick," Adele tattled. "He hasn't roasted it yet."

"What's sauce for the goose," Lorelei said as she tried to grab Russell's marshmallow.

Quickly, they were "fencing" with marshmallow-tipped sticks. Russell and Lorelei became the judges as they set up matches between the cousins. Arnie fought the boys, who gladly got on their knees to make for a fair fight.

After the final cry of "touché," they toasted the last few marshmallows and sat around the fire as it died down to mere embers. They sang "Shenandoah," "Shoo Fly," and ended the evening with Arnie's request, "Twinkle, Twinkle Little Star."

Russell poured water on the embers and Alan raked the

ground to guarantee they'd extinguished the fire entirely. Alan started coughing from the smoke.

Lacey giggled. "Don't pretend the smoke is bothering you. Lorelei is practically in a cloud of it, and she's not coughing."

"She's used to it." Russell stood with his arms akimbo and stared at her. The look in his eyes sent sparks through her. "Everyone knows smoke follows beauty."

ᔕ

Russell lay in his bed and closed his eyes. Instead of the hideous scenes of war that usually flashed across his mind, he pictured Lorelei with a speck of apple strudel on her lower lip. For the first time since he'd come home, he felt the knot in his chest loosen. He'd been able to horse around and laugh tonight—and it was because of Lorelei.

Arnie's cot squeaked as he tossed about in the little parlor. Accustomed to the little boy's restlessness, Mutt snuffled and settled back in. Lorelei had marked Arnie's height on the pantry doorframe this morning—just another one of her little ways of making sure Arnie felt secure about this being his new home. She'd made this old house a home with her warmth, laughter, and hard work.

The house creaked as it always did—the settling sounds of old timbers easing after the burden of a day. *Like I do.* He smiled wryly.

Somewhere in the house, someone coughed. Russell rolled over, yawned, and drifted off to sleep.

"Russell. Russell! Wake up." Lorelei stood over him, her beautiful hair streaming like ribbons down past her waist. She shook his shoulder again. Desperation tainted her sweet voice. "I need your help. It's Alan."

twenty

"There. That's better." Lorelei eased Beatrice back onto the pillows she'd piled beneath her shoulders to ease the coughing. Unsure if it made any difference, Lorelei still kept pillows piled beneath the shoulders and heads of four of the kids and Mrs. Diamond. They'd all come down with the flu in the past day and a half.

At first, Russell moved Alan into the nursery in an attempt to isolate him. By daybreak, all of the teens except Adele were also sick. They'd been brought here, too. Russell argued hotly with Lorelei that she shouldn't help, that she'd get sick, too. She'd turned around, made a gauze mask, and returned. Since then, he'd not been able to send her away. With the girls sick, Russell needed a woman to help with their care.

They'd transformed the big nursery into a sick ward. Mama kept Adele and Arnie away from the doorway and delivered broth, tea, and fresh linen and towels.

"S—sorry." Mrs. Diamond rasped after being violently ill.

"Shh. It is nothing." Lorelei supported her head and held a glass to her lips. "Sip. Rinse your mouth. You will feel better for it."

"I want my mama," Lacey whimpered in her fever-cracked voice.

Lorelei watched as Russell tenderly sponged her blue-tinged face and made soothing sounds. They'd been going from bed to bed, doing their best to control the fever, ease the cough, and keep their patients hydrated. When Russell first put up supplies, fearing the epidemic, he'd bought quinine and Aspirin. The posters in town advised using both, so they'd diligently dosed each patient.

By afternoon, everyone except Alan seemed stable. Lorelei knew from the newspapers that many who died of the ravaging disease did so within the first day. As long as she and Russell kept them medicated and hydrated, they ought to pull through—all except for Alan.

Russell sat by Alan's bedside, hollow-eyed with grief. From Alan's rattled, irregular breathing, Lorelei knew he had little time left unless God intervened. She went over and sat on the opposite side of the bed. Taking up a damp cloth, she fought tears as she sponged his parched, hot skin.

"Eternal Father, we've done our best. You know how we love Alan. Please, Lord, if it be Your will, heal this young man."

Alan opened his eyes. They were glazed, yet he feebly reached for Lorelei's hand. "God is love."

"Yes. Yes, God is love."

Russell made an agonized sound. He stood, paced away, and came back. Standing over the bed, he muttered, "This is my fault."

"No, Russell. You did your best. You tried to protect these children."

"I made him take half of that buck to the Rimmons. Rimmon's son brought milk today—because his father is down with the flu. If I hadn't been so stubborn and—"

"Stop! You were right to want a young man to be responsible for his actions, and you were right to share the meat with a family who needed it. Life isn't lived on our power. We aren't in control, and we don't bear responsibility for tragedies like this."

"Then God is to blame." Russell buried his head in his hands. "God allows the war; God allows illness." He lifted his face. "How can you serve Him when He refuses to protect His own children? Look at Alan. Just look at him!"

"I see a young man in God's hands." Her mask didn't successfully muffle her sob. "I want him to recover and sit at your table again, but if he does not, I know his heart is right with the Lord and I will someday feast with him in heaven. This, I cling to. It is the hope Jesus bought for us on the cross."

"That's where we're different—you still hope. Me? I've learned otherwise."

❧

"Leave him alone, Lori," Mama said softly.

"I can't." Lorelei slipped past her mother and headed toward the large oak tree. It was barren of leaves, and a fresh mound of dirt beneath it carried a lovingly made wooden cross that lay beside a small collection of old family headstones. The pastor had come out and performed the funeral. Russell refused to come inside after the burial. He'd been out there ever since, and sunset had given way to dusk, then the moon rose. Still, he stood alone beneath the barren branches, staring at the grave.

Lorelei said nothing at all. Leaves crunched beneath her shoes as she walked to his side and silently slipped her hand into his.

"It's too cold out here for you." Even as his words rejected her, his fingers curled about hers.

"My hand is warmer than yours."

"So is your heart. Go back inside, Lorelei. The chill inside me will freeze you. I've already caused enough heartache and damage."

"You've done no such thing."

He let out a gusty sigh and said nothing more.

"Come inside. Your mother needs to see you before she goes back to bed."

He cast a quick look at the second story of the house. "Her light's on. Your mom will take care of her. She'll sleep better in her own room tonight."

"I'll peek in on her during the night."

He looked down at her. "Just like you slip in to tug Arnie's covers up higher?"

"You knew I do that?"

"Buttercup, you're like a guardian angel around here. I don't think anyone does anything without you hovering over their shoulder." The gentle look on his face hardened. "But you can stop hovering over me. I'm a lost cause. God and I— we weren't on speaking terms before this happened." He gestured toward the fresh grave. "Now—well, now, it's plain as can be that He's cursed me for what I've done."

"God isn't that way, Russell. God is faithful. His character is unchanging. Bad things happen in life—things we cannot understand. They hurt, but God is with us during the hurt to give us consolation. If there is distance between you and Him, He is not the one who pulled away."

"That's some snappy theology you've worked out."

His words cut her to the core. Lorelei gulped, then closed her eyes. *Please, God, give me wisdom so I speak only the words You would have me say.*

"Lost, Buttercup? It's not easy to try to make sense of it all when things go wrong. I've given up. There's no use pursuing God when all He does is turn His back on me."

"God does not turn His back!" She staggered back from his bitter words. "You once told me you gave your heart to Jesus when you were a boy. So now you think to snatch it back because life is hard? Is that all a vow means to you?"

He glared at her stonily.

"Think of what a vow is. It does not say you will be true to your words only if all pleases you. I think of my parents. When they wed, they promised for better and worse, for richer and poor, in sickness and in health. When things were hard for them, they did not blame each other, pull apart, and curl in opposite corners. They clung together and gave their all."

"That's what marriage is."

"Yes. Two people make a promise to one another, and you expect them to keep their word. How can you think a vow made to God is less binding? You, Russell, made a vow to God. It was an eternal one—that no matter what life brought, you would follow Him. Instead of thinking of yourself, it is time for you to start serving Him."

"What more does He want?" Russell slashed the air with his hand in sheer frustration. "I've done everything I can. I deliver food. I dig graves. I've adopted an orphan."

"Your deeds are not what He wants. He wants your heart."

The air hissed out of his lungs. He flinched as if she'd struck him.

Lorelei watched the pain in his eyes. Even in the moonlight, the deep anguish he felt shone in them. She'd spoken the truth. The message wasn't a gentle one, and part of her wanted to soften the impact, but she couldn't water down the foundational truth. Until Russell chose to yield control to God, he'd fight a painful and losing battle.

After a prolonged silence, she murmured, "I left supper for you in the warming box." With a heavy heart, she walked back inside.

❧

In the next two weeks, Russell worked from first light to well after dark. Arnie, shaken by another death, trailed after him like a second shadow. His cousins all leaned on him to be strong. "You're like the Rock of Gibraltar," Philip said as Russell helped him back upstairs after his first meal at the family table.

A rock? I can't let them see that I'm like a million grains of shifting, sinking sand. They depend on me.

Even with all his hard work, Lorelei's words rang in his ears. *Your deeds are not what He wants. He wants your heart.*

One evening, he came back from delivering food in town to find Philip in the large parlor, working on refinishing a piece of furniture. At first, Russell couldn't see what it was. By the time he reached a decent vantage point, Philip turned. "I saw this in the attic and decided it needed to be repaired."

Russell stared at the burned altar.

The teen reverently ran his palm across the surface. "When I saw it, I felt closer to Alan." His voice cracked, "I remember his last words."

"'God is love,'" Russell remembered aloud.

Nodding his head, Philip started to sand the singed wood. Drawn to his side, Russell studied the damage. "We can fix it, can't we?"

"It won't be the same as new." Russell thumbed an edge. "I can plane it, and you could rout the edge. Then we can sand it to even out this other surface. A little putty and darker stain will cover any of the imperfections."

Late into the night, they worked on the altar. Every spare moment the next three days went toward restoring it. Finally, late at night, all alone, Russell ran a polishing cloth over the surface. Though he'd put Arnie to bed upstairs, the little guy had crept back downstairs and fallen asleep beneath Russell's jacket on a small sofa. Arnie stirred and sat up. He rubbed his eyes.

"Russell?"

"Yeah, Buddy?"

Arnie padded over and snuggled close. He wrapped his little arm around Russell's neck and curled his other hand around the edge of the altar. "Can we pray at this one, just like we do at the one in church?"

twenty-one

Russell's breath caught. *I'm not equipped to do this. God, why are You putting me in this position?* One look at Arnie's innocent eyes forced Russell to tamp down his own doubts. "Would you like to?"

Arnie nodded. He slithered onto his knees, folded his hands, and frowned. "I'm too short."

"Here." Russell knelt on one knee and crooked the other up. He lifted Arnie to sit on it, and the little boy then folded his hands and rested them on the altar.

"That's right," Arnie said happily. He closed his eyes tightly and dove right in. "God, it's me. Arnie. You got my daddy and mommy and baby 'Liz'beth with you. Please take good care of them. Russell takes good care of me. Night night. Amen."

"Amen." Russell hugged him tightly. "Now go on up to bed."

"Yessir."

Russell sat on the floor by the altar as despair washed over him. *If only my soul could be restored like this house and altar. If only my faith were that simple and pure.*

❧

"The paper in town says the flu is still bad, but it's not claiming as many folks as it did in October," Russell said when he got home one evening.

"How much longer will it last?" His mother took a sip of tea.

Russell shrugged. "No one can say."

"I want to go home," Beatrice said quietly. "It's been good of you to have us stay, but in the end, it didn't make any difference. I'm homesick." She laughed. "I'd even be glad to have Mama scold me for slacking on my chores."

Lorelei cut Arnie's meat and didn't participate in the conversation. The Diamonds needed to make this decision on their own.

"Going home by wagon is going to be too taxing," Russell said.

His mother nodded. "We'll go by train."

"Tomorrow is Sunday," Mama said.

"We'll leave Monday," Mrs. Diamond decided.

After everyone left the table, Russell remained, as had become his custom. Lorelei started to clear the dishes. "Mama and I will return to the cottage, too."

His head shot up. "Why?"

"Because it is time."

"Arnie needs you!"

Silently, Lorelei left him and went to the kitchen. Alone and up to her elbows in suds, she scrubbed a plate and fought back her disappointment. *Why couldn't you need me, Russell?* Tears stung her eyes and nose.

Mama came in, picked up a dishtowel, and started to dry dishes. "There was a time, I thought Russell was the answer to my prayers. You reminded me the pastor said we should pray specifically, and I did—just as you said—that God would put a husband for you on our cottage porch. Russell fixed that porch. I hoped with time, his heart would mend, too, Lori. It hasn't.

"You cannot be with a man who has hardened his heart against God. It is too hard for you to be under his roof and not set your affections on him. With his strength and kindness, he will woo you, but it is not what God would bless. On Monday, we will move back home, too."

Heart breaking, Lorelei whispered, "I know. I've already told him."

❧

"It's over!" Russell didn't bother to knock. He plowed straight into the cottage and repeated, "It's over!"

"What?"

He swept Lorelei up and swung her around. "The war! They declared Armistice! It's over!"

"Praise God!" Mama said from the kitchen doorway.

As Russell set Lorelei down, he still couldn't contain his relief. He held her shoulders and planted an exuberant kiss on her cheek. She gave him a shocked look, but he laughed and grabbed her mother in an enveloping hug. "It's done."

Arnie tugged on his slacks. "Do we get to sell-brate with marshmallows?"

"Better than that. We'll go to town. If you all promise to wear masks and stay away from others, we'll go in tomorrow. They're planning music in the park and a parade."

Arnie scratched his knee. "Daddy had mag'zines. They showed soldiers marching, marching, marching in parades. You gonna wear your soldier clothes, Russell?"

The question jolted him. Russell hadn't thought about his uniform since the night he'd happened across it before he left home. The very thought of ever putting it on again made him sick inside.

"The war is over, Arnie." Lorelei poked the little boy in the belly and made him laugh. "No more uniforms. What if we decorate the buggy? How would that be?"

"Terrific!"

Indeed, the buggy did look terrific. Russell chuckled as he hitched the geldings to it the next afternoon. "You folks out-did yourselves. This is the fanciest buggy in all of Virginia!"

Even the black crepe on doors and fresh graves in the cemetery didn't dampen spirits. Folks from all around came to town to revel in the good news. The gauze masks couldn't muffle the shouts of victory. The War to End All Wars was over. Never again would man engage in such brutality.

For the first time in months, Russell felt a glimmer of hope for the future.

❧

Lorelei carefully cleaned each piece of glass, then wrapped the edges with copper foil. Once the foil cupped the edges, she used her crimper to burnish it in place. She'd decided to do this window as a gift for Russell—a thanks for his generosity. The copper foil allowed her to make this far more intricate, and she'd constructed it so he could place it in the library window since he often slipped in that room when he needed to ponder matters.

"What are you up to now?"

His voice startled her. She jumped and let out a gasp.

"Sorry. I didn't mean to scare you. Hey—you cut yourself!"

"It's nothing." She set down the small piece of ruby glass and grabbed a rag. "I'm used to cutting myself. It's just part of the job."

He braceleted her wrist with his hand and turned the finger toward the light. "Poor finger. If this happened to Arnie, he'd want me to kiss it better."

"I'm not Arnie." She pulled away. A shiver ran through her, so she reached over and grabbed her sweater.

"No, you're not." Russell held the sweater for her. "I came over to talk with you about that."

"That I am not Arnie?" She glanced at her finger, decided it wasn't going to bother her and didn't need any bandaging, and set back to work on the window.

Russell chuckled. "No. Arnie's in with your mother. They get along famously."

"They do," Lorelei agreed. She tucked a finished piece in place and started to foil the edges of a deep green leaf.

"Will you please stop messing with that and look at me?"

Surprised at his request, she laid down the leaf and foil, then turned toward him.

"Arnie misses you up at the house. I miss you more."

His admission stunned her. Lorelei blinked at him in utter surprise.

Russell leaned forward. He traced her hairline with his forefinger and quietly said, "Buttercup, we've been through a lot together."

"We have." The tenderness in his touch and voice made her want to lean closer.

"I'm not very good with fancy words." He cupped her cheek. "But Lorelei, I can be myself around you. There isn't anyone else I can say that about. You listen and are honest about what you think. I don't know another gal in the world with a heart as big as yours."

"Russell, those are fancy words. Kind ones. Your praise means much to me."

His eyes darkened as he rubbed his thumb across her lips. "And my love? Does that mean much to you? I want to marry you, Lorelei."

She sucked in a shocked breath. His words thundered in her ears, made her world tilt crazily.

"Don't you love me, too?" His voice dropped an octave as he asked those words in a velvety voice.

The chill she'd felt earlier doubled. Lorelei stepped back and wrapped her arms around herself. "Yes. No." She shook her head. "Russell, it does not matter how I feel. My love for you is strong, but my love for God makes such a marriage impossible."

His brow furrowed. "What is that supposed to mean?"

Hot tears scorched down her cheeks. Everything inside trembled as she searched for the right words. "Russell, the man I marry must love God. In marriage, two become one. My heart and body tell me such a union would be wonderful, but my soul tells me no. We would not be a good match because there is this difference between us. Faith matters. It matters much."

"It doesn't have to. I'll go to church, if that's what bothers you. You can continue to say grace at meals and bring up our children with Bible reading." He got off the stool and came closer. Cupping her shoulders, he drew her close. "I wouldn't expect you to give up anything that is dear to you."

"But—"

"Your mother—she'd move in with us. She'll make a wonderful grandma for Arnie, don't you think?"

His words broke her heart. Lorelei pressed a hand to her mouth to hold back a sob.

He brushed away her tears. "Buttercup, this was supposed to be a happy moment. Things are looking up."

"My heart says yes, but my soul says no. Russell, you honor me with this proposal, but I cannot accept it. A woman should not marry a man in hopes of changing him. It is unwise. Though I love you, marriage would be wrong because the Lord is my Shepherd, but He is your enemy."

She could barely see him through her tears. Her legs felt rubbery, and she blindly reached behind herself for the table to keep herself from falling.

"If that's how you feel." Russell's voice sounded grim, muffled.

Instead of bracing her, the table slid. The sound of glass shattering filled her ears as the world tilted and everything went dark.

twenty-two

"Mom!" Russell burst into the cottage with Lorelei draped limply across his arms. Ever since he'd come to the realization that he loved Lorelei, he'd begun to think of her mother as his, too. The horror on her face cut him to the core. "She fainted. She's running a fever."

"Put her in bed. Go get the quinine and aspirin." Mrs. Goetz hurried into the bedroom and yanked back the covers.

By the time Russell returned, Lorelei was dressed in a lawn nightgown and covered by a sheet. Her mother worriedly sponged her wrists and face. "She is so hot. Too hot. Please, Russell, hold her up so I can make her take your medicine."

Of the people he'd seen with the flu, no one had been as sick as Lorelei—no one except Alan. Russell sat at the bedside, nearly crazed with grief. He couldn't bear to lose Lorelei. He trickled broth into her, held her head when she was sick, sponged her to control the fever. Nothing helped.

She grew weaker by the hour. Her coloring changed to the telltale bluish-white that indicated she didn't have long.

Russell stared at her and remembered when Alan was at this point. He'd whispered, "God is love."

Lorelei believed that, too. *My beautiful Lorelei, whose world is so full of light and color. Her soul sparkles with the joy of the Lord.*

What do I believe? He'd tried to make bargains with God in the trenches. *If You spare me and my buddy, I'll. . . Get me out of here and. . . Make this war end. . .* Now, he sat at the bedside of the woman he'd grown to love. His hands and heart were empty.

I can't bargain. I never could. I have nothing to offer God. I have no power. You are God, and I am a man—one who cannot bear to lose this woman.

Lorelei had spoken of vows and promises and commitment. *When things got rough, I failed to rely on the Lord. I tried to live on my own terms, and I turned on God. What kind of fool have I been?*

He took the Bible Lorelei kept at her bedside and started to read where a blue ribbon that was purpled with age lay between the pages in the eighth chapter of Mark:

And when he had called the people unto him with his disciples also, he said unto them, Whosoever will come after me, let him deny himself, and take up his cross, and follow me. For whosoever will save his life shall lose it; but whosoever shall lose his life for my sake and the gospel's, the same shall save it. For what shall it profit a man, if he shall gain the whole world, and lose his own soul? Or what shall a man give in exchange for his soul? Whosoever therefore shall be ashamed of me and of my words in this adulterous and sinful generation; of him also shall the Son of man be ashamed, when he cometh in the glory of his Father with the holy angels.

The words cut to the depths of his soul. He had nothing to exchange with God. . .nothing to give but a heart that was jaded and aching. The man in him wanted to bargain still—to beg God for this sweet woman's life—but that wasn't right. He couldn't make a deal with God. Sovereign, Almighty God owed him nothing. If in His grace He spared Lorelei, it would be a blessing beyond all hope, but if He didn't spare her. . .

Even then, I will serve You, Lord.

Russell slipped onto his knees. He closed both hands around Lorelei's and prayed. "Father, take my wayward heart and make it yours. I beg Your forgiveness for letting anger and pride separate me from You. Lord, I love this woman. I promise to follow You no matter what her fate. She'd said there was always the hope of eternity—of being seated together at the banqueting table in heaven. Our only hope now is in Your promise of eternity and salvation. Merciful God, be with us, I pray."

❧

Wrapped in her nightgown, two blankets, and propped in the corner of the couch, Lorelei swallowed the apple cider and hummed appreciatively.

"Thirsty, Buttercup?"

"Yes." She sipped more as Russell held the glass to her lips.

He sat next to her and played with the tip of her frazzled braid. "You're looking miles better."

She managed a weak laugh. "That is a terrible thing to say. As you carried me out here, I saw my reflection in the mirror. I'm a fright!"

"You're beautiful." He scanned her face slowly. "I need to tell you something."

Please, no. Please, Russell, don't ask me to marry you again. It nearly tore my heart out, telling you no last time. I'm too weak right now for this.

"While you were sick, I did a lot of soul searching. I didn't like what I saw. Things have changed. I've recommitted myself to God."

"Oh, Russell!"

"It's not supposed to make you cry." A lopsided grin tilted his mouth.

"They are happy tears."

His woodsy, masculine scent enveloped her as he leaned closer and used the corner of the sheet to dab her cheeks. His voice deepened. "Before you got sick, I told you I love you. Do you remember?"

She nodded slowly.

He looked into her eyes. "You were right to refuse my proposal. We wouldn't have had the bond in our marriage that God gives to His children."

"I didn't want to hurt you, Russell. I never wanted to hurt you."

"Shh. I know. Because you stood firm in your faith, you challenged me. It wasn't in a spirit of cruelty—you held up a mirror to my soul and forced me to look at myself."

"Since I met you, I've held a burden for you. God gave me a special passage to lean upon."

"Tell me."

She felt weak as water. Without her saying a word, Russell tucked her into his side and pressed her head to his shoulder. She closed her eyes at the security and serenity she felt in that moment, then recited softly, "It's in the first chapter of Second Corinthians. 'Blessed be God, even the Father of our Lord Jesus Christ, the Father of mercies, and the God of all comfort; Who comforteth us in all our tribulation, that we may be able to comfort them which are in any trouble, by the comfort wherewith we ourselves are comforted of God. For as the sufferings of Christ abound in us, so our consolation also aboundeth by Christ.'?"

"We've had plenty of tribulation. I'm ready for that comfort and consolation." He pressed a kiss to her temple. "Lorelei, my heart overflows with love for you. Will you marry me?"

"I love you, too, Russell. Being your wife would be an honor."

epilogue

"The altar is our something old," Lorelei told Russell's mother as she showed her the grand parlor where the wedding was to be held the next day. Once, it had been the workroom she and Russell shared. Now, it would serve as a wedding chapel.

Though outbreaks of the flu had lessened, quarantine laws made it impossible to use the church. Family members and a few close friends would come to the mansion for the nuptials, and Lorelei loved the fact that she and Russell would still have an altar for their wedding.

"And you have a beautiful new gown." Mrs. Diamond smiled.

"The something borrowed is Mama's lace hanky, and something blue is from Papa's Bible. I'm using the ribbon marker from it for my g—" She stopped abruptly as Russell entered the room. Heat suffused her cheeks at the thought that he'd almost overheard her speaking of such a thing.

"Everything set to your satisfaction?" He looked about.

"Not exactly." Mrs. Diamond's words shocked Lorelei. Walking toward her son, she said, "Lorelei thinks that beautiful altar is her something old. To my way of thinking, the bride is supposed to *wear* something old."

Russell wore a smug smile. "I've got that covered." He gave his mother a peck on the cheek; then she left the room. Russell took Lorelei's hand and tugged her to the window. A veritable rainbow of color shimmered around them from the stained glass. He pulled a frayed scarlet cord out of his pocket.

Three tiny hearts dangled from it.

"This has been in the family for seventy-seven years. I'd like you to tie it in your bridal bouquet. Maybe it's not exactly wearing it, but I think carrying it qualifies for the tradition."

"Three hearts. . .for God, you, and me?"

He smiled. "I knew you'd understand." He kissed her, then cupped her face in his hands and shook his head. "In the myth of Lorelei, she was a siren who called men to their destruction. You, my sweet siren, were the voice God used to call me to restoration."

The next afternoon, sun showered through the window onto the altar where they sealed their marriage with a heartfelt kiss.

"Now?" Arnie asked as he wiggled off to the side.

Lorelei laughed as Russell motioned for him to come. "Yes, now."

Arnie pulled two roses from Lorelei's bouquet and turned to the small crowd. "I got a s'prise. I'm 'dopted, so Rus—I mean, Dad—said I get to give these to my new grandmas."

They had a lovely wedding supper, and as a special celebration, that night, Russell arranged for fireworks to be shot off the main lawn for the guests' enjoyment. He and Lorelei stood by the window of their bedroom and held each other in the sparkling showers of light.

She walked her fingers up the buttons of his shirt. "It's Independence Day. I'd heard men think marriage takes away their freedom."

"Not this man." He captured her hand and kissed the backs of her fingers. "I've found liberty from the doubts and anger. It's not just the world that's at peace, Lorelei. I'm at peace."

"And I'm in love."

With a full heart and in a finished home that love had restored, he swept her into his arms and kissed her.

A Letter To Our Readers

Dear Reader:

In order that we might better contribute to your reading enjoyment, we would appreciate your taking a few minutes to respond to the following questions. We welcome your comments and read each form and letter we receive. When completed, please return to the following:

Fiction Editor
Heartsong Presents
PO Box 719
Uhrichsville, Ohio 44683

1. Did you enjoy reading *Restoration* by Cathy Marie Hake?
   ❏ Very much! I would like to see more books by this author!
   ❏ Moderately. I would have enjoyed it more if

   _____

   _____

   _____

2. Are you a member of **Heartsong Presents**? ❏ Yes ❏ No
   If no, where did you purchase this book? _____

   _____

3. How would you rate, on a scale from 1 (poor) to 5 (superior), the cover design? _____

4. On a scale from 1 (poor) to 10 (superior), please rate the following elements.

   ____ Heroine   ____ Plot
   ____ Hero   ____ Inspirational theme
   ____ Setting   ____ Secondary characters

5. These characters were special because?_____

_____

_____

6. How has this book inspired your life?_____

_____

_____

7. What settings would you like to see covered in future
   Heartsong Presents books? _____

_____

_____

8. What are some inspirational themes you would like to see
   treated in future books? _____

_____

_____

9. Would you be interested in reading other **Heartsong
   Presents** titles?   ❑ Yes   ❑ No

10.   Please check your age range:
      ❑ Under 18   ❑ 18-24
      ❑ 25-34   ❑ 35-45
      ❑ 46-55   ❑ Over 55

Name_____

Occupation_____

Address_____

City_____ State_____ Zip_____

Presents

Great Inspirational Romance at a Great Price!

Heartsong Presents books are inspirational romances in contemporary and historical settings, designed to give you an enjoyable, spirit-lifting reading experience. You can choose wonderfully written titles from some of today's best authors like Peggy Darty, Sally Laity, Tracie Peterson, Colleen L. Reece, Debra White Smith, and many others.

When ordering quantities less than twelve, above titles are $2.97 each.
Not all titles may be available at time of order.

$\mathcal{H}$EARTSONG ❤ PRESENTS

Love Stories
Are Rated G!

That's for godly, gratifying, and of course, great! If you love a thrilling love story but don't appreciate the sordidness of some popular paperback romances, **Heartsong Presents** is for you. In fact, **Heartsong Presents** is the premiere inspirational romance book club featuring love stories where Christian faith is the primary ingredient in a marriage relationship.

Sign up today to receive your first set of four, never-before-published Christian romances. Send no money now; you will receive a bill with the first shipment. You may cancel at any time without obligation, and if you aren't completely satisfied with any selection, you may return the books for an immediate refund!

Imagine. . .four new romances every four weeks—two historical, two contemporary—with men and women like you who long to meet the one God has chosen as the love of their lives. . .all for the low price of $10.99 postpaid.

To join, simply complete the coupon below and mail to the address provided. **Heartsong Presents** romances are rated G for another reason: They'll arrive Godspeed!

YES! Sign me up for Hearts❤ng!

NEW MEMBERSHIPS WILL BE SHIPPED IMMEDIATELY!
Send no money now. We'll bill you only $10.99 post-paid with your first shipment of four books. Or for faster action, call toll free 1-800-847-8270.

NAME_____

ADDRESS_____

CITY_____ STATE_____ ZIP_____

MAIL TO: HEARTSONG PRESENTS, P.O. Box 721, Uhrichsville, Ohio 44683
or visit www.heartsongpresents.com